Marx Machiavelli Chesterton Emerson Joyce Abbott Hardy Montaigne Cooper Austen Defoe Melville Haggard Hugo Eliot Grimm Stoker Carroll Christie Molière Wilde Maupassant Byron Engels Schiller Garnett Einstein Fitzgerald Smith Goethe Hawthorne Kafka Cotton Dostoyevsky Hall Baum Kipling Doyle Willis Leslie Dumas Henry Nietzsche Flaubert Turgenev Balzac Stockton Vatsyayana Crane Burroughs Whitman Verne Curtis Tocqueville Gogol Vinci Homer Widger Tolstoy Busch Darwin Thoreau Potter Freud Zola Twain Plato Scott Lawrence Kant Jowett Stevenson Dickens Andersen Cervantes Burton Hesse Harte London Descartes Voltaire Poe Aristotle Wells Hale James Hastings Cooke Bunner Shakespeare Richter Chambers Irving Doré Swift Dante Chekhov da Shaw Wodehouse Benedict Alcott Pushkin Newton tredition®

tredition was established in 2006 by Sandra Latusseck and Soenke Schulz. Based in Hamburg, Germany, tredition offers publishing solutions to authors and publishing houses, combined with worldwide distribution of printed and digital book content. tredition is uniquely positioned to enable authors and publishing houses to create books on their own terms and without conventional manufacturing risks.

For more information please visit: www.tredition.com

TREDITION CLASSICS

This book is part of the TREDITION CLASSICS series. The creators of this series are united by passion for literature and driven by the intention of making all public domain books available in printed format again - worldwide. Most TREDITION CLASSICS titles have been out of print and off the bookstore shelves for decades. At tredition we believe that a great book never goes out of style and that its value is eternal. Several mostly non-profit literature projects provide content to tredition. To support their good work, tredition donates a portion of the proceeds from each sold copy. As a reader of a TREDITION CLASSICS book, you support our mission to save many of the amazing works of world literature from oblivion. See all available books at www.tredition.com.

Project Gutenberg

The content for this book has been graciously provided by Project Gutenberg. Project Gutenberg is a non-profit organization founded by Michael Hart in 1971 at the University of Illinois. The mission of Project Gutenberg is simple: To encourage the creation and distribution of eBooks. Project Gutenberg is the first and largest collection of public domain eBooks.

The Iron Rule Or, Tyranny in the Household

Timothy Shay Arthur

Imprint

This book is part of TREDITION CLASSICS

Author: Timothy Shay Arthur
Cover design: Buchgut, Berlin – Germany

Publisher: tredition GmbH, Hamburg - Germany
ISBN: 978-3-8424-2728-0

www.tredition.com
www.tredition.de

The intention of the TREDITION CLASSICS series is to make world literature in the public domain available in printed format. Literary enthusiasts and organizations, such as Project Gutenberg, worldwide have scanned and digitally edited the original texts. tredition has subsequently formatted and redesigned the content into a modern reading layout. Therefore, we cannot guarantee the exact reproduction of the original format of a particular historic edition. Please also note that no modifications have been made to the spelling, therefore it may differ from the orthography used today.

THE IRON RULE;

OR, TYRANNY IN THE HOUSEHOLD.

BY

T. S. ARTHUR,

AUTHOR OF "LOVE IN HIGH LIFE," "LOVE IN A COTTAGE," "MARY MORETON; OR, THE BROKEN PROMISE," "AGNES; OR, THE POSSESSED,"
"INSUBORDINATION," "LUCY SANDFORD," "THE ORPHAN CHILDREN,"
"THE DEBTOR'S DAUGHTER," "THE DIVORCED WIFE," "PRIDE AND PRUDENCE,"
"THE TWO MERCHANTS," "CECILIA HOWARD," "THE BANKER'S WIFE," ETC.
COMPLETE IN ONE VOLUME.

Philadelphia:
1853

THE IRON RULE;

OR, TYRANNY IN THE HOUSEHOLD.

CHAPTER I.

ANDREW HOWLAND belonged to that class of rigid moralists who can tolerate in others no wanderings from the right way. His children were forced into the straight jacket of external consistency from their earliest infancy; and if they deviated from the right line in which they were required to walk, punishment was sure to follow.

A child loves his parent naturally. The latter may be harsh, and unreasonable; still the child will look up to him in weak dependence, while love mingles, like golden threads in a dark fabric, amid the fear and respect with which he regards him. Thus it was with the children of Andrew Howland. Their mother was a gentle, retiring woman, with a heart full of the best affections. When the sunshine fell upon her golden locks in the early days of innocence, it was in a home where the ringing laugh, the merry shout, and the wild exuberance of feeling ever bursting from the heart of childhood were rarely checked; or, if repressed, with a hand that wounded not in its firm contraction. She had grown up to womanhood amid all that was gentle, kind and loving. Transplanted, then, like a tender flower from a sunny border, to the cold and formal home of her husband, she drooped in the uncongenial soil, down into which her heart-fibres penetrated in search of nutrition. And yet, while drooping thus, she tenderly loved her husband, and earnestly sought to overcome in herself many true impulses of nature to which he gave the false name of weaknesses. It was less painful thus to repress them herself, than to have them crushed in the iron hand with which he was ever ready to grasp them.

Let it not be thought that Andrew Howland was an evil minded man. In the beginning we have intimated that this was not so. He purposed wrong to no one. Honest he was in all his dealings with the world; honest even to the division of a penny. The radical fault of his character was coldness and intolerance. Toward wrong-doing and wrong-doers, he had no forbearance whatever; and to him that strayed from the right path, whether child or man, he meted out, if in his power, the full measure of consequences. Unfortunately for those who came within the circle of his authority, his ideas of right and wrong were based on warped and narrow views, the result of a defective religious education. He, therefore, often called things wrong, from prejudice, that were not wrong in themselves; and sternly reacted upon others, and drove them away from him, when he might have led and guided them into the paths of virtue.

The first year of Andrew Howland's married life was one of deep trial to the loving young creature he had taken from her sunny home to cherish in his bosom—a bosom too cold to warm into vigorous life new shoots of affection. And yet he loved his wife; loved her wisely, as he thought, not weakly, nor blindly. He saw her faults, and, true to his character, laid his hands upon them. Alas! how much of good was crushed in the rigid pressure!

To Mr. Howland life was indeed a stern reality. Duties and responsibilities were ever in his thoughts. Pleasure was but another name for sin, and a weakness of character an evil not to be tolerated.

Enough, for our present purpose, can be seen of the character of Andrew Howland in this brief outline. As our story advances, it will appear in minuter shades, and more varied aspects. Seven years from the day of his marriage we will introduce him to the reader.

"What *shall* I do with this boy?" said Mr. Howland. He spoke sternly, yet in a perplexed voice, while he walked the floor of the room with a quickness of tread unusual. "If something is not done to break him into obedience he will be ruined."

"He needs all our forbearance," Mrs. Howland ventured to remark, "as well as our care and solicitude."

"Forbearance! I have no forbearance toward wrong, Esther. You have forborne until the child is beyond your control."

"Not entirely," was meekly answered, as the mother's eyes drooped to the floor.

At this moment a servant, who had been sent for the child, came in with him. A few doors away lived another child, about the same age, of whom little Andrew was very fond, and whose companionship he sought on every occasion. Against the father of this child Mr. Howland had imbibed a strong prejudice, which was permitted to extend itself to his family. Rigid and uncompromising in everything, he had observed that Andrew was frequently in company with the child of this neighbor, and felt impelled to lay a prohibition on their intercourse. But Andrew, a light-hearted, high-spirited boy, who inherited from his father a strong will, was by no means inclined to yield a ready obedience in this particular. He loved his little companion, and never was happier than when in her society. Naturally, therefore, he sought it on every occasion, and when the positive interdiction of their intercourse came, the child felt that a duty was imposed upon him that was impossible of fulfillment. Young as he was, he could endure punishment, but not give up his little friend. Advantage was therefore taken of every opportunity to be with her that offered. Punishments of various kinds were inflicted, but they acted only as temporary restraints.

As to this little girl herself, let it be understood, Mr. Howland had no personal objection. He had never seen anything that was wrong in her, and had never heard a word of evil spoken against her. The simple, yet all-embracing defect that appertained to her was his dislike of her father; and this dislike had its chief foundation in a wrong estimate of his character, the result of his own narrow prejudices. Somewhat hastily, we will admit, did Mr. Howland utter the word that was to separate the little friends, and the word was half-repented of as soon as spoken. But once uttered, it was a law to which he required the most implicit obedience. He thought not of the wrong the separation might do his child; he thought only of enforcing obedience—of breaking a stubborn will. Obedience in children was, in his eyes, everything—and he visited, with the sternest displeasure, every deviation therefrom. The consequence was, that his little ones, in their nest at home, rarely saw in the face of their father a smile of affection; rarely heard his voice in words of tenderness. Something, in their conduct was ever displeasing to him, and he attempted its correction by coldness, repulsion, harsh words, or cruel punishment. He never sought to lead, but to force them into the right way.

The word of interdiction was uttered, but Andrew could not give up his sweet little friend; and the word was therefore disregarded. Stealthily, to avoid punishment, he went to her but watchful eyes were upon him, and he was soon brought back. Gently and earnestly his mother would chide his disobedience; harshly his father would punish it—but all was of no avail.

"Where is Andrew?" asked Mr. Howland, on returning home one evening from his store, and not seeing the bright little fellow in the room with his mother. This was on the occasion of his introduction to the reader.

"I don't know. He was here just now," replied Mrs. Howland.

"I saw him a little while ago playing on the steps with Emily Winters," said the nurse, who had come recently into the family, and was not aware of the prohibition that existed in regard to the child she had mentioned.

"Is it possible!" exclaimed Mr. Howland, angrily. Then he added in an excited voice, "go and bring him home immediately!"

The nurse left the room and soon returned with the child. In his face was a look of blended fear, anger and resolution.

"Where have you been, sir?" sternly asked Mr. Howland.

The child made no answer.

"Do you hear me, sir?"

A slight motion of shrinking and alarm might have been seen in the little fellow as the angry voice of his father fell upon his ears. But he did not look up or make a reply.

"Will you answer me? Stubborn boy!" exclaimed Mr. Howland, now catching hold tightly of Andrew's arm.

"Why don't you answer your father, my child?" said the mother, in a voice that was tender and appealing. The tone reached the boy's heart, and he lifted his large blue eyes from the floor and fixed them on his father's threatening countenance.

"Say! Where have you been?" repeated Mr. Howland.

"To see Emily," returned Andrew.

"Haven't I forbidden you to go there?"

The child's eyes sunk again to the floor.

"Say! Haven't I forbidden you to go there?"

But there was no answer.

"Do you hear me?"

"Andrew! Andrew! why don't you answer your father?" came in distressed and tremulous tones from his mother's lips.

Mr. Howland was about turning to chide sharply his wife for this interference, when Andrew again raised his eyes and said—

"Yes, sir."

"Then why have you disobeyed me?"

The boy's eyes fell again, and he remained silent.

"I'll break you of this if I break your heart!" said Mr. Howland severely, and, as he spoke, he almost lifted the child from the floor with his strong arm as he led him from the room. A groan issued from the mother's heart and she covered her face and wept.

By the time Mr. Howland reached the chamber above, to which he repaired with Andrew, the excitement of his anger had subsided; but not his stern purpose in regard to his child, who had again disobeyed him. The absolute necessity of obedience in children he recognized in all its length and breadth. He saw no hope for them in the future unless obedience were constrained at every cost. Happy both for them and himself would it have been if he had been wiser in his modes of securing obedience, and more cautious about exacting from his children things almost impossible for them to perform.

Without a law there is no sin. Careful, then, should every parent be how he enacts a law, the very existence of which insures its violation.

Mr. Howland had sought, by various modes of punishment, other than chastisement, to enforce obedience in this particular case. Now he was resolved to try the severer remedy. Andrew had expected nothing farther than to be shut up, alone, in the room, and to go, perhaps, supperless to bed, and he was nerved to bear this without a murmur. But when the rod became suddenly visible, and was lifted above him in the air, his little heart was filled with terror.

"Oh, father!" he exclaimed, in a voice of fear, while his upturned, appealing face became ashy pale.

"You have disobeyed me again, my son," said Mr. Howland, coldly and sternly, "and I must whip you for it. Disobedient children have to be punished."

"Oh, father! Don't whip me! Don't!" came huskily from the lips of the terrified child. But even while he thus pleaded, the smarting strokes began to fall.

"Now, sir!" at length said Mr. Howland, pausing with the rod uplifted, "will you go into Mr. Winters' again?"

The child hesitated, and down came a blow upon his tender limbs, followed by the words—

"Say! Will you go in there any more?"

Still there was a reluctance to make this promise, and another and harder stroke was given. The father was resolved to conquer, and he did conquer. A promise was extorted from the child's lips, while, his heart yielded nothing.

"Very well, sir! See that you keep your word," said Mr. Howland, as he released the writhing sufferer from his firm grasp. "If you disobey me again in this thing, I will give five times as much."

And he turned from the chamber leaving the wronged and suffering child alone.

"I've begun now, and I'll go through with it," muttered Mr. Howland, as he reentered the room where his wife was sitting. "I never saw so perverse and self-willed a child in my life. If he is not subdued now, and forced to obey, his ultimate destruction is inevitable."

"His fault was not a very great one," Mrs. Howland ventured to suggest.

"Do you call disobedience a little fault?" asked Mr. Howland, his brow contracting as he spoke.

"I did not mean that," quickly answered Mrs. Howland. "I meant his going in to see Emily Winters. The children are very fond of each other."

"But I have told him not to go in there, haven't I?"

"Yes."

"Very well. That settles the matter. If he goes, he disobeys me; and if he disobeys me, he must be punished."

"But, Andrew— "

"It is useless to argue about this with me, Esther. Entirely useless. In your weakness you would indulge and ruin the boy. But I know my duty better."

Mrs. Howland sighed deeply and remained silent. Some ten minutes afterwards, seeing her husband engaged with a book, she arose and left the room. As soon as she closed the door, every movement was suddenly quickened, and she sprung up the stairway to the chamber from which had come down to her the screams of her boy, as he shrunk under the cruel strokes inflicted by the hand of his father. Entering, she saw Andrew sitting on the floor, with his arms resting on a low chair, and his face buried in them. He raised his head slowly, and turned to see who had come in. The instant he saw that it was his mother, a flush came into his pale face, and tears dimmed the light of his beautiful, tender, loving eyes. In another moment he was sobbing on her bosom.

"Dear Andrew must not be disobedient again," said the mother, so soon as her child had grown calm, bending close to his cheek as she spoke, and letting her breath fall warmly over it.

"Emily is a good little girl, and I love her. She ain't bad, mother. She is better than I am," quickly returned the child, raising himself up, and lifting his eyes earnestly to his mother's face.

"But your father has forbidden you to go to her house, Andrew."

"Won't he let Emily come to see me?" urged the child.

"No, dear. He wants you to play with some one else."

"But I don't want to play with any one else. Emily is a good girl, and I like her so much. Indeed she ain't bad, mother. She's good."

"I know, dear," answered the perplexed mother. "I know that Emily is a good girl. But— "

"Then why won't father let me play with her?" was Andrew's quick interrogation.

"He doesn't wish you to do so, my child, and you must be an obedient, good little boy, and then your father will love you."

"He don't love me!" said Andrew in a tone and with an emphasis that startled his mother.

"Oh yes, he does! He loves you very much. Isn't he your father?" replied Mrs. Howland in an earnest voice.

"He wouldn't have whipped me so hard if he had loved me! I'm sure he wouldn't, mother."

And tears gushed from the eyes of the child at the remembrance of his father's stern face, and the pain he had suffered.

"Andrew musn't speak so of his father," said Mrs. Howland in a chiding voice. "Andrew was disobedient; that was the reason why his father punished him. Andrew must be a good boy."

"I ain't bad, mother," sobbed the child. "I'm sure it ain't bad to play with Emily. She never does anything naughty."

"It is bad if your father forbids your doing so," replied Mrs. Howland.

"No—it can't be bad to play with Emily," said the little fellow, speaking half to himself. "She's so good, and I love her."

All in vain proved the mother's effort to make her boy see that it was wrong to play with Emily. He wanted a reason beyond the command of his father, and that she was not able to give. The more she talked with him, the more plainly did she see that rebellion was in his young heart, and that he would act it out in the face of all consequences. Deeply saddened was she at this conviction, for she well knew that obedience to parents is the good ground into which the seeds of civil and religious obedience in manhood must be sown.

As for herself, Mrs. Howland had no objection to little Emily Winters as the companion of Andrew. She was, as the boy said, a good girl, and her influence over him was for good. But the stern prejudice of Mr. Howland had come in to break up the friendship formed between the children, and his inflexible will would brook no opposition. All must bend to him, even at the risk of breaking.

Nearly half an hour did Mrs. Howland pass alone with her boy, striving to awaken the better impulses of his heart, and as they became active, seeking to implant in his mind a willingness to deny himself, in order to obey his father. But the father asked too much. There was no charge of evil against Emily as a reason for this interdiction. All the mother could say, was—

"It is your father's wish and command, my child, and you must obey him."

But this could not satisfy the boy's mind in a case where his feelings were so deeply interested. At length, Mrs. Howland turned to leave the room. Andrew followed her to the door, and looking up with a sad light in his large eyes, murmured—

"I do love you, mother!"

A tear fell upon his face as his mother stooped to kiss him. A little while after, and he was alone.

"I'm afraid," said Mrs. Howland, joining her husband soon after, "that we have done wrong in prohibiting all intercourse between Andrew and little Emily Winters."

"Why so?" was quickly asked, and in no very pleasant tone of voice.

"The children are very much attached to each other."

"That is no reason."

"It would be no reason if there was anything bad about Emily. But there is not. She is a very good little girl."

"I'm not so sure of that," said Mr. Howland.

"I never saw anything out of the way in her."

"It's more than I can say of her father, then," was replied. "There lies my chief objection. I want no intercourse between the families, and do not mean to have any. In this I am entirely in earnest. Andrew must seek another playfellow."

"I'm afraid we will have a great deal of trouble," sighed Mrs. Howland.

"I am not, then. Let me know whenever he disobeys in this matter, and I'll apply the remedy in a way to cure him. His will has to be broken, and the present occasion is as good as any other for effecting so all-important an object. The stronger he is tempted to disobey, the more effectual will be the subjugation of his will, when the conquest is made."

It was useless for Mrs. Howland to argue with her husband. He never yielded the smallest assent to any reasons she might bring, nor to any position she might assume. So, with a pressure on her heart, and a clear perception in her mind that he was wrong, she heard these last words in silence.

"Shall I call Andrew down?" asked the mother, as the tea-bell rung, soon after.

"No," replied Mr. Howland, firmly; "I wish him to understand that I am in earnest."

"Don't you think he has been punished sufficiently?" said Mrs. Howland, timidly.

"Of course I do not, or I would remit the penalty of transgression," coldly returned her husband. "He's a stubborn, self-willed boy, and must be made to feel that he has a master."

"Kindness and persuasion often does— "

"I will hear no more of that!" quickly returned Mr. Howland; "and I wish you, once for all, to understand, Esther, that I will not consent to an interference on your part with what I believe to be my duty. Thousands of children have been ruined by this weak kindness and persuasion, but this shall never be the case with mine."

Mr. Howland did not observe that his wife caught her breath, as he uttered the first few words of his harsh report. She made no further answer, but passed on with her husband to the tea-room. But she ate nothing. Dreamily rested her eyes on vacancy, as she sat at the table. Her mind took no note of images pictured on the retina, for her thoughts were in another place, and with her inner vision she saw the sad form of her wronged and suffering child shrinking in the lone chamber where he had been banished.

"Shall I take Andrew some supper?" she asked, as she arose, at length, from the table.

"He can have some bread and water," was coldly and briefly answered.

Will any one blame the mother, that she went beyond this? A few minutes afterward she entered the room in which Andrew had been punished, bearing in her hands a small tray, on which was a cup of milk and water, some toast, and a piece of cake. The twilight had already fallen, and dusky shadows had gathered so thickly that the eyes of Mrs. Howland failed to see her child on first entering the room.

"Andrew!" she called, in a low, tender voice.

But there was no reply.

"Andrew!"

Still all remained silent.

More accustomed to the feeble light that pervaded the chamber, Mrs. Howland now perceived her boy in a corner, sitting upon the floor, with his head reclining upon a low ottoman. He was asleep. Placing the tray she had brought upon a table, Mrs. Howland lifted the child in her arms, and as she did so, he murmured in a sad voice—

"Don't, papa! oh, don't strike so hard!"

Unable to repress her feelings, the mother's tears gushed over her cheeks, and her bosom heaved with emotions that spent themselves in sobs and moans.

For many minutes she sat thus. But the child slept on. Once or twice she tried to awake him, that he might get the supper she had brought; but he slept on soundly, and she refrained, unwilling to call him back to the grief of mind she felt that consciousness would restore. Undressing him, at length, she laid him in his bed, and bending over his precious form in the deeper darkness that had now fallen, lifted her heart, and prayed that God would keep him from evil. For a long time did she bend thus over her boy, and longer still would she have remained near him, for her heart was affected with an unusual tenderness, had not the cries of her younger child summoned her from the room.

CHAPTER II

THE tears of childhood are soon dried. Grief is but as the summer rain. On the next morning, little Andrew's voice was heard singing over the house, as merrily as ever. But the sound did not affect, pleasantly, the mind of his father. He had not forgotten the scene of the previous evening, and was far from having forgiven the disobedience he had punished so severely. Had Andrew come forth from his chamber silent and with a sober, abashed, and fearful countenance, as if he still bore the weight of his father's displeasure, Mr. Howland would have felt that he had made some progress in the work of breaking the will of his child. But to see him moving about and singing as gaily as a bird, discouraged him.

"Have I made no impression on the boy?" he asked himself.

"Father!" said Andrew, running up, with a happy smile upon his face, as these thoughts were passing through the mind of Mr. Howland, "won't you buy me a pretty book? Oh! I want one— "

"Naughty, disobedient boy!"

These were the words, uttered sternly, and with a forbidding aspect of countenance, that met this affectionate state of mind, and threw the child rudely from his father.

Andrew looked frightened for a moment or two, and then shrunk away. From that time until his father left the house, his voice was still. During the morning, he amused himself with his playthings and his little sister, and seemed well contented. But after dinner he became restless, and often exclaimed—

"Oh! I wish I had somebody to play with!"

At length, after sitting by the window and looking out for a long time, he turned to his mother, and said—

"Mother, can't I go and see Emily Winters?"

"No, Andrew, of course not," replied Mrs. Howland.

"Why, mother? I like her, and she's good."

"Because your father doesn't wish you go to her house. Didn't he punish you last evening for going there?"

At this the child grew impatient, and threw himself about with angry gestures. Then he sat down and cried for a time bitterly, while his mother strove, but in vain, to soothe him. For hours his thoughts had been on his little friend, and now he cared for nothing but to see her. Denied this privilege from mere arbitrary authority, his mind had become fretted beyond his weak ability to control himself.

It was, perhaps, an hour after this, that Mrs. Howland missed Andrew, and fearful that he might have been tempted to disobey the command laid upon him, raised the window and looked into the street. Just as she did so, she saw him running back toward his home from the house of Mr. Winters, on the steps of which sat Emily. Entering quickly, she heard him close the street-door with a slight jar, as if he designed making as little noise as possible.

"Where have you been, Andrew?" asked Mrs. Howland as soon as he came up to her room, which he did soon after.

"Down in the kitchen with Jane," was replied without hesitation.

"Have you been nowhere else?" Mrs. Howland repented having asked this question the moment it passed her lips, and still more when the child answered as unhesitatingly as before, "No, ma'am."

Here was falsehood added to disobedience! Poor Mrs. Howland turned her face away to grieve and ponder. She found herself in a narrow path, and doubtful as to the steps to be taken. She said nothing more, for she could not see clearly what it was best for her to say; and she did nothing, for she could not see what it was best for her to do. But she resolved to be watchful over her boy, lest he should again be tempted into disobedience.

The mother's watchfulness, however, availed not. Ere night-fall Andrew was with his little friend again. Unfortunately for him, the pleasure he derived from her society caused him to forget the passing of time, and his stolen delight was, in the end, suddenly dispelled by the stern voice of his father, who passed the door of Mr. Winters on his way homeward.

Slowly and in fear did the child obey the angry command to return home. He knew that he would be punished with great severity, and he was not mistaken. He was so punished. But did this avail anything? No! On the next day he asked his mother to let him sit at the front door.

"I'm afraid you'll go into Mr. Winters," said Mrs. Howland, in reply.

"Oh, no; indeed I won't, mother," was the ready answer.

"If you disobey me, I can't let you go to the door again."

"Oh, I won't disobey you," replied the child.

"Very well, Andrew, I'll trust you. Now, don't deceive me."

The child promised over and over again, and Mrs. Howland trusted him. Ten minutes afterward she looked out, but he was nowhere to be seen. A domestic was sent to the house of Mr. Winters, where Andrew was found, as happy as a child could be, playing with his little friend Emily. On being reproved by his mother for this act of disobedience, he looked earnestly in her face and said—

"You won't tell father, will you? He'll whip me so, and I don't like to be whipped."

"But why did you go in there?" said Mrs. Howland. "Haven't we forbidden you? And didn't you promise me that if I'd let you go to the front door, you would stay there?"

"I couldn't help it, mother," replied Andrew.

"Oh, yes, you could."

"Indeed I couldn't, mother. I saw Emily, and then I couldn't help it."

There was an expression in the child's voice as he said this, that thrilled the feelings of his mother. She felt that he spoke only the simple truth—that he could not help doing as he had done.

"But Andrew must help it," she was constrained to reply. "Mother can't let him go to the front door again."

"You won't tell father, will you?" urged the child, lifting, earnestly, his large, bright, innocent eyes to his mother's face. "Say, you won't tell him?"

Grieved, perplexed, and troubled, Mrs. Howland knew not what to say, nor how to act.

"Dear mother!" urged the boy, "you won't tell father? Say you won't?" And tears began to glisten beneath his eyelids.

"Andrew has been disobedient," said the mother, trying to assume an offended tone. "Will he be so anymore?"

"If you won't tell father, I'll be good."

The mother sighed, and fixed her gaze musingly on the floor. Her thoughts were still more confused, and her mind in still greater perplexity. Ah, if she only knew what was right!

"I will not tell your father this time," she at length said, "but don't ask me, if you are again disobedient."

But of what avail was the child's promises. He had strong feelings, a strong will, and, though so very young, much endurance. A law, at variance almost with a law of his nature, had been arbitrarily enacted, and he could not obey it. As well might his father have shut him up, hungry, in a room filled with tempting food, and commanded him not to touch or taste it. Had an allegation of evil conduct been brought against Emily Winters; had any right reason for the interdiction been given, then Mr. Howland might have had some power over the strong will and stronger inclinations of the child. But into the mind of Andrew, young as he was, came a sense of injustice and wrong on the part of his father, and there was no willingness, from filial duty, to yield obedience in a case where every feeling of his heart was at variance with the command.

The struggle so early commenced between the father and his child, was an unceasing one. The will of Andrew, which by other treatment might have been bent to obedience, gained a vigor like the young oak amid storms, in the strife and reaction of his daily life. Instead of drawing his child to him, there was ever about Mr. Howland a sphere of repulsion. Andrew was always doing something to offend his father; and his father was in consequence always offended. A kind word from paternal lips rarely touched the ears of the boy, and, but for the love of his gentle mother, home would have been almost intolerable. Steadily, against all opposition, chidings, and punishment, Andrew would seek the company of his little friend Emily on every convenient occasion. To avoid the consequences he would practice deception, and utter direct falsehood without compunction or hesitation. At last, after a struggle of two years, even the father became wearied and discouraged at the perseverance of his child; and there came a suggestion to his mind, that probably, to continue as he had been going on for so long a time, would do more harm than good. It requires no little self-denial for a man like Andrew Howland to yield in such a contention, and let the will of his child remain unbroken. But, after a long debate with himself, his better conviction triumphed over prejudice and the tenacity of a mind fixed in its own opinions. He ceased to command obedience in the case of Emily Winters, and therefore ceased to punish Andrew on her account. Nevertheless, he rarely saw him in her company that the displeasure he felt was not manifested by a frown, or some word that smote painfully upon the ear of his child.

Possessing an active, independent mind, Andrew failed not to excite the displeasure of his father in many ways. In fact he was always in disgrace from some cause or other and the subject of angry reproof, harsh judgment, or direct punishment. Often his conduct needed reproof and even punishment; but he was the victim of such frequent wrong judgment and unjust reproof and punishment, that by the time he was eleven years of age, he looked upon his father more as a persecuting tyrant than a kind parent, who sincerely desired his good. An instance of wrong judgment and unjust punishment we will here give.

As Andrew grew older and formed school boy associations, his impulsive and rather reckless character brought him frequently into collision with his companions, and he gained a reputation which was by no means good. Every now and then some one would complain to Mr. Howland of his bad conduct, when he, taking all for granted, would, without investigation, visit the offence with severe punishment.

One day, when in his twelfth year, as Andrew was at play during a recess in the school hour, a boy larger than himself made an angry attack upon a lad much below him in size, and was abusing him severely, when Andrew, acting from a brave and generous impulse, ran to the rescue of the smaller boy, and, in a sudden onset, freed him from the hands of his assailant. Maddened at this interference, the larger boy turned fiercely upon him. But Andrew was active, and kept out of his way. Still the larger boy pursued him, using all the while the most violent threats. At length finding that he was likely to be caught and get roughly handled, Andrew took up a stone, and drawing back his hand, warned the boy not to approach. He continued to approach, however, vowing, as he did so, that he would beat the life half out of him. True to his word, and in self-defence, Andrew threw the stone, which struck the boy full on the forehead and knocked him down. For some minutes he lay stunned and half-insensible. Frightened at the consequences of his act, Andrew sprung to the side of the fallen lad and tried to raise him up. Failing in this he ran for the teacher, who was in the school-room. A little cold water thrown into the boy's face revived him, when he went home to his parents. The teacher made careful inquiries into the matter, which satisfied him that Andrew was not very greatly to blame.

A short time after this occurrence, a gentleman entered the store of Andrew's father, and said, with much excitement of manner,

"Mr. Howland! I've come to make complaint against that boy of yours."

"Against Andrew?"

"Yes, sir. He's nearly killed my son!"

"Bless me!" exclaimed Mr. Howland, in a distressed voice. "What has happened? How did he do it?"

"Why, sir! without the slightest provocation, he took up a large stone and struck my boy with it on the forehead, knocking him down senseless. I have had to send for the doctor. It may cost him his life."

"Oh dear! dear! What will become of that boy?" exclaimed Mr. Howland, wringing his hands, and moving up and down the floor uneasily. "Knocked him down with a stone, you say?"

"Yes sir And that without any provocation. I can't stand this. I must, at least, protect the lives of my children. Every week I have had some complaint against your son; but I didn't wish to have a difficulty, and so said nothing about it. But this is going a little too far. He must have a dreadful temper."

"There is something very perverse about him," remarked Mr. Howland, sadly. "Ah, me! What am I to do?"

"There may have been some slight provocation," said the man, a little modified by the manner in which his complaint was received, and departing from his first assertion.

"Nothing to justify an assault like this," replied Mr. Howland with promptness. "Nothing! Nothing! The boy will be the death of me."

"Caution him, if you please, Mr. Howland, against a repetition of such dangerous conduct. The result might be deplorable."

"I will do something more than caution him, you may be sure," was answered, and, as he spoke, the lips of Mr. Howland were drawn tightly across his teeth.

The man went away, and Mr. Howland dispatched a messenger to the school for Andrew immediately, and then started for home. He had been there only a little while, when the boy came in with a frightened look. To his father's eyes conscious guilt was in his countenance.

"Go up stairs, sir!" was the stern salutation that met the lad's ears.

"Father, I— "

"Silence, sir! Don't let me hear a word out of your head!"

The boy shrunk away and went up to his own room in the third story, whither his angry father immediately followed him.

"Now, sir, take off your jacket!" said Mr. Howland who had a long, thick rattan in his hand.

"Indeed father," pleaded the child, "I wasn't to blame. Bill Wilkins— "

"Silence, sir! I want none of your lying excuses! I know you! I've talked to you often enough about quarreling and throwing stones."

"But, father— "

"Off with your jacket, this instant! Do you hear me?

"Oh, father! Let me speak! I couldn't— "

"Not a word, I say! I know all about it!" silenced the pleading boy. His case was prejudged, and he was now in the hands of the executioner. Slowly, and with trembling hands, the poor child removed his outer garment, his pale face growing paler every moment, and then submitting himself to the cruel rod that checkered his back with smarting welts. Under a sense of wrong, his proud spirit refused to his body a single cry of pain. Manfully he bore his unjust chastisement, while every stroke obliterated some yet remaining emotion of respect and love for his father, who, satisfied at length with strokes and upbraiding, threw the boy from him with the cutting words—

"I shall yet have to disown you!" and turning away left the apartment.

CHAPTER III.

WHILE Mr. Howland yet paced the floor in a perturbed state of mind, after the severe flogging he had given to Andrew, and while he meditated some further and long-continued punishment for the offences which had been committed, a servant handed him a note. It was from Andrew's teacher, and was to this effect—

"From careful inquiry, I am entirely satisfied that your son, when he threw the stone at William Wilkins, was acting in self-defence, and, therefore, is blameless. Wilkins is a quarrelsome, overbearing lad, and was abusing a smaller boy, when your son interfered to protect the latter. This drew upon him the anger of Wilkins, who would have beaten him severely if he had not protected himself in the way he did. Before throwing the stone, I learn that Andrew made every effort to get away; failing in this, he warned the other not to come near him. This warning being disregarded, he used the only means of self-protection left to him. I say this in justice to your son, and to save him from your displeasure. As for Wilkins, I do not intend to receive him back into my school."

For a long time Mr. Howland remained seated in the chair he had taken on receiving the teacher's note. His reflections were far from being agreeable. He had been both unjust and cruel to his child. But for him to make an acknowledgment of the fact was out of the question. This would be too humiliating. This would be a triumph for the perverse boy, and a weakening of his authority over him. He had done wrong in not listening to his child's explanation; in not waiting until he had heard both sides. But, now that the wrong was done, the fact that he was conscious of having done wrong must not appear. In various ways he sought to justify his conduct. At length he said, half aloud—

"No matter. He deserved it for something else, and has received only his deserts. Let him behave himself properly, and he'll never be the subject of unjust censure."

It was thus that the cold-hearted father settled, with his own conscience, this question of wrong toward his child. And yet he was a man who prayed in his family, and regularly, with pious observance, attended upon the ordinances of the church. In society he was esteemed as a just and righteous man; in the church as one who lived near to heaven. As for himself, he believed that severity toward his boy, and intolerance of all the weaknesses, errors, and wayward tendencies of childhood, were absolutely needed for the due correction of evil impulses. Alas! that he, like too many of his class, permitted anger toward his children's faults to blind his better judgment, and to stifle the genuine appeals of nature. Instead of tenderness, forbearance, and a loving effort to lead them in right paths, and make those paths pleasant to their feet, he sternly sought to force them in the way he wished them to go. With what little success, in the case of Andrew, is already apparent.

Angry at the unjust punishment he had received, the boy remained alone in his room until summoned to dinner.

"He doesn't want anything to eat," said the servant, returning to the dining-room where the family were assembled at the table.

"Oh, very well," remarked the father, in a tone of indifference, "fasting will do him good."

"Go up, Anna," said Mr. Howland to the servant "and tell him that I want him to come down."

That word would have been effectual, for Andrew loved his mother; but Mr. Howland remarked instantly:

"No, no! Let him, remain. I never humor states of perverseness. If he wishes to fast he can be gratified."

Mrs. Howland said no more, but she took only a few mouthfuls of food while she sat at the table. Her appetite was gone. After dinner she went up to Andrew's room with a saucer of peaches and cream. The moment she opened the door the lad sprung toward her, and while tears gushed from his eyes, he said—

"Indeed, indeed, mother, I was not to blame! Bill Wilkins was going to beat me—and you know, he's a large boy."

"But you might have killed him, Andrew," replied the mother, with a gentle gravity that, in love, conveyed reproof. "It is dangerous to throw stones."

"I had to defend myself, mother. I couldn't let him beat me half to death. And I told him to keep off or I would strike him with the stone. I'm sure I wasn't to blame."

"Why, was he going to beat you, Andrew? What did you do to him?" asked Mrs. Howland.

"I'll tell you, mother," replied the boy. "He was pounding with his fist a poor little fellow, not half his size, and I couldn't stand and see it if he was a bigger boy than me. So I took the little boy's part; and then he turned on me and said he'd beat the life out of me. I ran from him and tried to get away, but he could run the fastest, and so I took up a stone and told him to keep off. But he was mad, and wouldn't keep off. So I struck him with it, and, mother, I'd do it again to-morrow. No boy shall beat me if I can defend myself."

"Why didn't you tell your father of this?" asked Mrs. Howland.

"I tried to tell him, but he wouldn't listen to me," said the lad, with ill-concealed indignation in his voice. "And he never will listen to me, mother. He believes every word that is said against me, and flogs me whether I am guilty or not. I'm sure he hates me!"

"Hush! hush my boy! don't say that. Don't speak so of your father."

"Well, I'm sure he don't love me," persisted Andrew.

"Oh, yes, he does love you. He only dislikes what is wrong in you. My son must try to be a good boy."

"I do try, mother; I try almost every day. But somehow I do wrong things without thinking. I'm always sorry at first; sorry until father begins to scold or whip me, and then I don't seem to care anything about it. Oh, dear! I wish father wasn't always so cross!"

While Andrew thus talked, his tears had ceased to flow; but now they gushed over his cheeks again, and he leaned his face upon his mother's bosom. Mrs. Howland drew her arms closely around her unhappy boy, while her own eyes became wet. For many minutes there was silence. At last she said, in a kind, earnest voice—

"I've brought you a nice saucer of peaches and cream, Andrew."

"I don't want them, mother," replied the lad.

"You'll be hungry before night, dear. It's nearly school-time now, and you'll get nothing to eat until you come home again."

"I don't feel at all hungry, mother."

"Just eat them for my sake," urged Mrs. Howland.

Without a word more Andrew took the saucer.

"Ain't they nice?" asked Mrs. Howland, as she saw that her boy relished the fruit and cream.

"Yes, dear mother! they are very good," replied Andrew; "and you are good, too. Indeed I love you, mother!"

The last sentence was uttered with visible emotion.

"Then, for my sake, try and do right, Andrew," said Mrs. Howland, tenderly.

"I will try, mother," returned the boy. "I do try often; but I forget myself a great many times."

Soon after Andrew started for school. On arriving, his teacher called him up and said—

"Did your father get my note?"

"I don't know, sir," replied Andrew.

"What did he say to you?"

The boy's eyes sunk to the floor and he remained silent.

"I sent your father a note immediately," said the teacher, "telling him that you were not to blame."

Andrew looked up quickly into his teacher's face, while a shadow fell upon his countenance.

"You don't know whether he received it?"

"No sir."

The teacher called up another lad, and inquired if he had delivered the note given him at the dwelling of Mr. Howland, as directed. The boy replied that he had done so.

"Very, well. You can take your seat."

Then turning to Andrew, the teacher said—

"Was it about William Wilkins that your father sent for you?"

"Yes, sir."

"You told him how it was?"

The boy was silent.

"He didn't punish you, surely?"

Tears trembled on the closing lashes of the injured child; but he answered nothing. The teacher saw how it was, and questioned him no farther. From that time he was kinder toward his wayward and, too often, offending scholar, and gained a better influence over him.

Not for a moment, during the afternoon, was the thought that his father knew of his blamelessness absent from Andrew's mind. And, when he returned home, his heart beat feverishly in anticipation of the meeting between him and his parent. He felt sure that the teacher's note had reached his father after the punishment had been inflicted; and he expected, from an innate sense of right and justice, that some acknowledgment, grateful to his injured feelings, of the wrong he had suffered, would be made. There was no thought of triumph or reaction against his father. He had been wrongly judged, and cruelly punished; and all he asked for or desired was that his father should speak kindly to him, and say that he had been blamed without a cause. How many a dark shadow would such a gleam of sunshine have dispelled from his heart. But no such gleam of light awaited his meeting with his father, who did not even raise his eyes to look at him as he came into his presence.

For awhile Andrew lingered in the room where his father sat reading, hoping for a word that would indicate a kinder state of feeling toward him. But no such word was uttered. At length he commenced playing with a younger brother, who, not being able to make him do just as he wished, screamed out some complaint against him, when Mr. Howland looked up, suddenly, with a lowering countenance, and said, harshly—

"Go out of the room, sir! I never saw such a boy! No one can have any peace where you are!"

Andrew started, and made an effort to explain and excuse himself, for he was very anxious not to be misunderstood again just at this time. But his father exclaimed, more severely than at first.

"Do you hear me, sir! Leave this room instantly!"

The boy went out hopeless. He felt that he was unloved by his father. Oh! what would he not have given—what sacrifice would he not have made—to secure a word and a smile of affection from his stern parent, whom he had known from childhood only as one who reproved and punished.

CHAPTER IV.

WRONGED and repelled, Andrew left the presence of his father, sad, hopeless, yet with a sense of indignation in his heart against that father for the wrong he had suffered at his hands.

"It's no use for me to try to do right," he murmured to himself. "If I want to be good, they won't let me."

As these thoughts passed through his mind, a feeling of recklessness came over him, and he said aloud—

"I don't care what I do!"

"Don't you, indeed?"

The voice that uttered this sentence caused him to start. It was the voice of his father, who had left his room soon after the expulsion of Andrew, and was at the moment passing near, unobserved by the boy.

"Don't care what you do, ha!" repeated Mr. Howland, standing in front of the lad, and looking him sternly in the face. "You've spoken the truth for once!"

For nearly a minute Mr. Howland stood with contracted brows, scowling upon the half-frightened child. He then walked away, deeply troubled and perplexed in his mind.

"What is to become of this boy?" he said to himself. "He really seems to be one of those whom Satan designs to have, that he might sift them as wheat. I sadly fear that he is given over to a hard heart, and a perverse mind—one predestinated, to evil from his birth. Ah me! Have I not done, and am I not still doing everything to restrain him and save him! But precept, admonition, and punishment, all seem, thrown away. Even my daily prayers for him remain unanswered. They rise no higher than my head. What more can I do than I am now doing? I have tried in every way to break his stubborn will, but all is of no avail."

While Mr. Howland mused thus, Andrew, oppressed by the sphere of his father's house, was passing out at the street door, although expressly forbidden to go away from home after his return from school. For some time he stood leaning against the railing, with a pressure of unhappiness on his heart. While standing thus, a lad who was passing by said to him—

"Come, Andy! there's a company of soldiers around in the Square. Hark! Don't you hear the music? Come! I'm going."

This was a strong temptation, for Andrew loved music and was fond of sight-seeing. It would be useless, he knew, to ask the permission of his father, who usually said "No," to almost every request for a little liberty or privilege. Especially at the present moment would the request of this kind be useless.

"Come, Andy! come!" urged the boy, for Andrew, restraining the first impulse to bound away at the word soldiers, was debating the question whether to go or not.

Just then the air thrilled with a wave of music, and Andrew, unable longer to control himself, sprung away with his companion. For half an hour he enjoyed the music and military evolutions, and then returned home.

"Where have you been, sir?" was the sharp question that greeted him as he came in.

"Around in the Square, to see the soldiers," replied Andrew.

"Who gave you permission to go?"

"No one, sir. I heard the music, and thought I'd just go and look at them a little while. I've not been doing anything wrong, sir."

"Wrong! Isn't disobedience wrong? Haven't I forbidden you, over and over again, to leave the house after school without my permission? Say! You don't care what you do! That's it! Go off up stairs with you, to your own room, and you'll get nothing but bread and water until to-morrow morning! I'll teach you to mind what I say!"

The boy went sadly up to his room. It had been a day of severer trial than usual—of greater wrong and outrage upon him as a child. For the time his spirit was broken, and he wept bitterly when alone in his silent chamber, that was to be his prison-house until the dawn of another day.

"Where is Andrew?" asked Mrs. Howland, as her little family gathered at the supper table, and she found that one was missing.

"I've sent him up to his room. He can't have anything but bread and water to-night," replied Mr. Howland, in a grave tone.

"What has the poor child done, now?" inquired the mother, in a troubled voice.

"He went off to see the soldiers, though he had been expressly forbidden to leave the house after coming home from school."

"Oh, dear! He's always doing something wrong—what will become of him?" sighed the mother.

"Heaven only knows! If he escape the gallows in the end, it will be a mercy. I never saw so young a child with so perverse an inclination."

"Andrew had no dinner to-day," said Mrs. Howland, after a little while.

"His own fault," replied the father, "he chose to fast."

"He must be very hungry by this time. Won't you allow him something more than bread and water?"

"No. If he is hungry, that will taste sweet to him."

Mrs. Howland sighed and remained silent. After supper, she took food to her boy. A slice of bread and a glass of water were first placed on a tray, and with these the mother started up stairs. But, ere she reached the chamber, her heart plead so strongly for the lad, that she paused, stood musing for a few moments, and then returned to the dining-room. A few slices of tongue, some biscuit, bread and butter, and a cup of tea were taken from the table, and with these Mrs. Howland returned up stairs. Unexpectedly, her husband met her on the way.

"Who is that for?" he asked, in a voice of surprise, seeing the articles Mrs. Howland was bearing on the tray.

"It is Andrew's supper," was replied; and as Mrs. Howland said this, her eyes drooped, abashed beneath the stern and rebuking gaze of her husband.

"Esther! Is it possible!" exclaimed Mr. Howland. "Didn't I say that Andrew must have nothing but bread and water for his supper?"

"He has had no dinner," murmured the mother.

"I don't care if he had nothing to eat for a week. I said he should have only bread and water, and I meant what I said. Esther! I am surprised at you. Of what avail will be efforts at correction, if you counteract them in this way?"

Mrs. Howland never contended with her husband. In all expressed differences of opinion, it was his habit to bear her down with an imperious will. She was weak, and he was her strong tyrant. Not a word more did she speak but returned to the dining-room, and replaced the food she had prepared for Andrew by simple bread and water.

The feelings of childhood never run for a long time in the same channel. Very soon after entering his room, Andrew's mind lost its sad impression, and began to search about for something to satisfy its restless activity. First he got upon the chairs, and jumped from one to another. This he continued until his feet passed through the slender cane-works of one of them. Then he turned somersets on the bed, until more than a handful of feathers were beaten out and scattered about the room. Next he climbed up the posts and balanced himself on the tester, to the no small risk of breaking that slender frame work, and injuring himself severely by a fall. Soon the compass of the room became too narrow, and the elevation of the bed-posts too trifling for his expanding ideas. He went to the window, and, opening it, looked forth. Here was a new temptation. The roof of a piazza, built out from a second story, came up to within a foot of the window-sill. He had often ventured upon this roof, and he sprung out upon it again without a moment's hesitation or reflection, and running along, with the lightness of a cat, gained the roof of the back building, which he ascended to the very apex, and then placed himself astride thereof. Here he sat for some minutes looking around him and enjoying the prospect. On the end of the back building was fastened a strong pole, running up into the air some ten feet. On the top of this pole was a bird-box, in which a pair of pigeons had their nest. Two young pigeons had been hatched out, and now nearly full-fledged and ready to fly, they were thrusting their glossy heads from the box, and looking about from their airy height.

A fluttering of wings, as the mother-bird returned with food for her young ones, attracted the attention of Andrew, and looking up, he saw the young pigeons. Instantly came a desire to remove them from their nest. But the way to that nest was too difficult and perilous for him to think of securing his wish. This was the first impression. Then he fixed his eye on the nest, and watched the old bird, as she sat on a ledge that projected from the box, while she distributed to her younglings the food she had brought. Thus sat the boy at the moment his mother left the dining-room with the comfortable supper she had prepared for him, and there she would have found him in comparative safety, had she not been prevented from carrying out the kind promptings of her heart.

The longer Andrew gazed at the young birds, the more desirous did he become to get them in his possession. Over and over again he measured the height and thickness of the pole with his eyes, calculating, all the while, his ability to climb it, and the amount of danger attendant on the adventure.

"I'm sure I could do it," said he, at length rising from the place where he sat and walking with careful step to the edge of the roof, at the point above which the pole projected. Grasping the pole firmly, he first leaned his body over until he could see in a perpendicular line to the pavement in the yard below, a distance of more than forty feet. For a moment his head swam, as he looked from the dizzy height; but he shut his eyes and clung to the pole until self-possessed again. Then he looked up at the bird-box and reaching his hands far above his head, grasped the pole firmly and drew his body a few inches, upward. Clinging tightly with his legs to retain the slight elevation he had acquired, he moved his hands farther along the pole, and then drew himself higher up. Thus he progressed until he had reached a point some five or six feet above the roof, when his strength became exhausted, and, unable to retain even the position he had acquired, his body slowly descended the pole, swinging around to the side opposite the roof. On reaching the bottom it was as much as he could do to get himself once more in a position of safety, where he stood for a few moments, until he could recover himself. He then tried the ascent again. This time he nearly reached the box, when his strength once more failed him, and he had to slide down the pole as before. But Andrew was not a lad to give up easily anything he attempted to do. Difficulties but inspired him to new efforts, and he once more tried to effect the perilous ascent, firmly resolved to reach the box at the third trial. In his eagerness, he became unconscious of all danger, and commenced clambering up the pole with as much confidence as if it had been placed on the ground.

Great violence had been done to the feelings of Mrs. Howland by her husband. His stern rebuke hurt her exceedingly. She did not feel that she was doing wrong in yielding to the appeals of her heart in favor of her wayward, ever-offending boy. Her mother's instinct told her, that he needed kindness, forbearance, and frequent exemption from punishment; and she felt that it was better for him to have this, even though in gaining it for him she acted in violation of her husband's wishes and command—yea, even though her child knew that such was the case. Sadly was she aware of the fact, that the father's iron-handed severity had nearly crushed affection out of the heart of his child; and that all obedience to him was extorted under fear of punishment. And she well knew that her interference in his favor, while it could not estrange him from his father more than he was already estranged, would give her greater influence over him for good. Such were the conclusions of her mind—not arrived at by cold ratiocination, but by woman's shorter way of perception. And she knew that she was right.

Hurt in her own feelings was she, by her husband's harsh, rebuking words, and sad for the sake of her boy, as she returned to the dining-room. For some time she remained there, debating with herself whether she should stealthily convey something more than the bread and water to Andrew, or take him the meager supply of food his father had ordered. In the end her feelings triumphed. A large slice of cake and an apple were placed in her pocket. Then with the bread and water she went up to her son's chamber.

"Bless me! what a boy!" fell from the lips of Mrs. Howland, as she pushed open the door and saw the disordered condition of the room. The chairs were scattered about the apartment, and through the caning of one of them was a large hole. The wash-bowl and pitcher were on the floor, and a good deal of water spilled around. The bed-clothes were nearly all dragged off; and it was plain, from the feathers scattered about, that Andrew had been amusing himself with jumping on the bed. Lifting her eyes to the tester, Mrs. Howland saw nearly a yard of the valance torn away and hanging down.

"Oh, what a boy!" she again murmured. "He seems possessed with a spirit of mischief and destruction. Andrew!"

She called the lad's name, but there was no answer.

"Andrew! where are you?" The mother looked searchingly about the room. But she neither saw the boy nor heard his voice. Perceiving now that the back-window was open, she sprung to it with a sudden thrill of alarm. The first object that caught her sight, was Andrew suspended in the air on the pole that supported the pigeon-box. He was just about reaching the object of his perilous adventure. A wild scream of terror came from the mother's lips, ere she had time to think of self-control. The scream, as it pierced suddenly the ears of Andrew, startled and unnerved him. A quick muscular exhaustion followed, and ere he could recover from the confusion and weakness of the moment, his hands were dragged from their hold, and he went flashing down from the eyes of his mother like the passing of a lightning gleam. Another scream thrilled on the air, and then Mrs. Howland sunk swooning to the floor.

Mr. Howland was just stepping into the yard, when his son fell, crushed by the terrific fall, at his feet.

"Oh, father!" came in a voice of anguish from the yet conscious boy, as he lifted one hand with a feeble effort toward his parent. Then a deathly whiteness came ever his face, and he fainted instantly.

On the arrival of a physician it was found that Andrew's left arm was broken in two places, his left ancle dislocated, and two ribs fractured. As to the internal injury sustained, no estimate could be made at the time. He did not recover fully from the state of insensibility into which he lapsed after the fall, until the work of setting the broken bones and reducing the dislocation was nearly over. His first utterance was to ask for his mother. She was not present, however. Her cries, at seeing the peril and fall of her child, brought a domestic to the room, who found her lying insensible upon the floor. Assistance being called, she was removed to her own chamber, where she remained, apparently lifeless for the space of half an hour. When she recovered, her husband was pacing the chamber floor with slow, measured steps, and his eyes cast down.

"Andrew! Is he dead?" were her first words. She spoke in a low voice, and with forced composure.

Mr. Howland paused, and approached the bed on which lay his pale exhausted wife, just awakened from her death-like unconsciousness.

"No, Esther. He is not dead," was calmly replied.

"Is he badly hurt"?

The mother held her breath for a reply.

"Yes, badly, I fear," answered Mr. Howland, in the same calm voice.

"Will he live?" almost gasped the mother.

"God only knows," replied Mr. Howland. Then glancing his eyes upward piously, he added, "If it be His will to remove him, I— "

"Oh, Andrew! don't say that!" quickly exclaimed the mother. "Don't say that!"

"Yes, Esther, I will say it," returned Mr. Howland, in a steady voice. "If it be His good pleasure to remove him, I will not murmur. He will be safer *there* than here."

"Oh, my poor, poor boy!" sobbed Mrs. Howland. "My poor, poor boy! To think that he should come to this? Oh, it was wrong to send him off as he was sent! to punish him so severely for a little thing. Heaven knows, he had suffered enough, unjustly, without having this added!"

"Esther!" exclaimed Mr. Howland, "this from you!"

The distressed mother, in the anguish of her mind, had given utterance to her feelings, with scarce a thought as to who was her auditor. The sternly uttered words of her husband subdued her into silence.

"I did not expect this from you, Esther," continued Mr. Howland, severely, "and at such a time."

And he stood looking down upon the mother's pale face with a rebuking expression of countenance. Mrs. Howland endured his gaze only for a few moments, and then buried her face in the bedclothes. Her husband, as his eyes remained fixed upon her form, saw that it was agitated by slight convulsions, and he knew that she was striving to suppress the sobs in which her heart was seeking an utterance. For a little while he stood looking at her, and then retired, without speaking, from the chamber, and sought the one where the physician was yet engaged with Andrew. The lad was insensible when he left him a short time before; now signs of returning animation were visible.

"Mother!—mother! Where is mother?" he at last said, opening his eyes, and glancing from face to face of those who were gathered around him.

"You have nearly killed your mother," replied. Mr. Howland, expressing, without reflection, the feeling of anger toward the lad that was still in his heart.

An instant change was visible in the countenance of Andrew; a change that caused the physician to turn suddenly from his patient and say, in a low, severe tone—

"Sir! Do you wish to murder your child?"

Mr. Howland felt the rebuke, yet did not his eyes sink for a moment beneath the steady gaze of the physician, who, after a moment's reflection, added—

"Pray, sir, don't speak to your child in this way at the present time. It may be as much as his life is worth. If he have done wrong, his punishment has been severe enough, Heaven knows! How is his mother?"

"Better. She has recovered from her faintness," replied Mr. Howland.

The door opened while he was yet speaking, and Mrs. Howland came in, looking pale and agitated. The physician raised his finger to enjoin prudence, and then turning to Andrew said, in a cheerful voice,

"Here is your mother, my boy."

Mrs. Howland came quickly to the bedside. As she bent over to kiss the white-faced sufferer, the child sobbed out—

"Oh mother!—dear mother!"

The mother's frame quivered under the pressure of intense feeling, and she was on the eve of losing all self-control, when the physician whispered in her ear.

"Be calm, madam—the life of your child may depend on it!"

Instantly the mother was calm in all that met the eye. Close to her child she bent, and with a hand laid gently on his clammy forehead, she spoke to him words of comfort and encouragement, while the physician proceeded in the work of bandaging his broken and injured limbs.

As for Mr. Howland, he walked the floor with compressed and silent lips, until the physician's work was done. He pitied the suffering boy, yet there was nothing of what he called weakness in his pity. The idea that Andrew was suffering a just retribution for his wrong conduct, was distinctly present to his mind. And he even went so far as to put up a prayer that the pain he was enduring, and must for a long time endure, might work in him a salutary change—might lead to his reformation.

In due time the poor boy was made as comfortable as the nature of his injuries would permit, and quiet and order restored to the agitated family.

"You see, my son, that punishment always follows evil conduct." These were the first words spoken by Mr. Howland to his suffering boy, as soon as he found himself alone with him. And then he lectured him on disobedience until the poor child grew faint.

CHAPTER V.

THE boy recovered, in due time, from his injuries, but there was no manifest change in his character, nor was there any relaxing of the iron hand of authority with which his father sought to hold him back from evil. It is no matter of wonder that he grew hardened and reckless as he grew older; nor that, to avoid punishment, he sought refuge in lying, secretiveness, and deceit.

The other children—there were three beside Andrew—being different in character, were more easily subdued under the imperious will of their father, whom they feared more than they loved. Assuming, in his own mind, that Andrew's will had been permitted to gain strength ere an effort had been made to control it, Mr. Howland resolved not to fall into this error in the case of the children who followed; and, assuredly, he did not. Through the rigors of unfailing punishment for every act of wrong-doing, they were forced into the way he would have them go, and though rebellion was often in their hearts, it was rare, indeed, that it found its way into act, except when there was the utmost certainty that their misconduct would not be found out. Thus they learned to act hypocritically toward their father, and to regard him as one who marred, instead of promoting their pleasure.

Mr. Howland had one son besides Andrew—one son and two daughters. Mary was next to Andrew, Edward came next to her, and Martha was the youngest. Edward resembled his father more than any of the other children. He was cold and calm in his temperament, and little inclined to be drawn aside by the restless, vagrant spirits that were ever luring Andrew from the strict line laid down for him by his father. Daily perceiving the great value attached by his father to external propriety of conduct, Edward made a merit of what to him was easy. This vexed Andrew, who had opportunities for knowing all about the worth of Edward's apparent excellencies, and he sneeringly applied to him the epithet of "Saint," which was the cause of his drawing down upon himself, in more than one instance, the displeasure of his father. But he had become so used to censure and reproof, that it had little influence over him. Let him do wrong or right, he was almost sure to be harshly judged, and he had, by the time he was sixteen, almost ceased to care what others thought of his conduct.

Mary, whose age was next to that of Andrew, failed to acquire any influence over her brother. She had been fretful and peevish as a child, and he had worried her a great deal, and, in consequence, received frequent punishment on her account. This tended naturally to disunite them, and make them cold toward each other. Instead of Mr. Howland striving, as their mother ever did, to reconcile their difficulties, and make them friends, he would listen to Mary's complaints against Andrew, and mark his displeasure by reproof or punishment. Trifles, that would have been in a little time forgotten and forgiven, were raised into importance by the stern father, and sources of unhappiness and enmity created out of the most ordinary, childish misunderstandings. Thus, in his mistaken efforts to destroy what was evil in his children, he was only rooting the evils he would remove more deeply in the groundwork of their minds. Instead of harmonizing, his actions had the constant effect of disuniting them. Brotherly love and sisterly affection had small chance for growth in the family over which he presided.

For all this, out of his family Mr. Howland was highly respected and esteemed. He had the reputation of being one of the most upright, just, and humane men in the community; and many wondered that he should have so bad a son as Andrew, whose reputation abroad was little better than at home. At school he was almost constantly involved in quarrels with other boys; and, from the immediate neighborhood of Mr. Howland, complaints frequently came of his bad conduct and reckless annoyances toward neighbors. In truth, Andrew was a bad boy; self-willed and overbearing toward his companions; a trespasser on the rights and privileges of others; and determinedly disobedient to his father. But for all this his father was to blame. While sternly repressing the evil in his child, he had not lovingly sought to develop the good. While vainly striving to root out the tares which the enemy had sown, he had injured the tender wheat, whose green blades were striving to lift themselves to the sunlight. Alas! how many parents, in their strange blindness, are doing the same work for their unhappy children.

Amid all the perverseness that marked the character of Andrew; amid all his hardness and wrong-doing; his attachment to Emily Winters remained as pure and earnest at sixteen, as when a child he suffered punishment rather than give up her society. Emily, who was about his own age, had grown, by this time, into a tall, graceful girl, and was verging on toward womanhood with a rapidity that made the boy's heart tremble as he marked the distance which an earlier development of body was placing between him and the only one, except his mother, that he had ever loved.

Between the families of Mr. Howland and Mr. Winters there was no intercourse. Mr. Howland early imbibed a strong prejudice against Mr. Winters, who did not happen to be a church member, and who, on that account, was believed by Mr. Howland to be capable of doing almost any wrong action, if tempted thereto. Certain things done by Mr. Winters, who was independent in his modes of thinking and acting, had been misunderstood by Mr. Howland, or judged by one of his peculiar standards of virtue. From that time he was considered a bad man; and, although Mrs. Winters, who was a woman beloved by all that knew her, called upon Mrs. Howland when the family of the latter came into the neighborhood, Mr. Howland positively forbade a return of the call. Less obedient to his arbitrary commands did he find his son. Andrew formed an early friendship for little Emily, and sought every opportunity, spite of restriction and punishment, to enjoy her society.

This was continued until the children grew to a size that caused the parents of Emily to observe the attachment as one far from being agreeable to them, and to feel desirous of drawing a line of separation between their daughter and a boy so notoriously bad as Andrew Howland. When the children were twelve years old, they felt bound to take some action in the case, and began by giving Andrew a gentle hint, one day, to the effect that his visits to their house were rather too frequent. This was enough for the high-spirited boy. He left, with a burning spot on his cheek, vowing, in his indignation, that he would never enter their door again, nor speak to Emily. But it was much easier to keep the first part of this promise than the last. As early as the next day he met Emily on his way to school. She was going to school also, and had much farther to, walk than himself. To enjoy her society, he went with her all the way. This made him late, and he was in consequence, kept in by the teacher, half an hour after his own school was dismissed. But this punishment did not deter him from repeating the act on the next day and on the next. From that time he rarely came to school until ten or fifteen minutes after the session was opened; and, sometimes, Emily was late also. Reproof and punishment doing no good, the teacher sent a note to Andrew's father, complaining of his want of punctuality. A severe reprimand was the consequence. This failing of the desired effect, the boy was put on bread and water for days at a time. But complaints from the teacher still arriving, corporeal punishment was added. No change, however, followed. In the end Andrew was sent home from school as incorrigible.

"What shall I do with the boy!" was the despairing exclamation of Mr. Howland, when this event occurred. "Idleness will complete his ruin, and he is too young to put out."

"I will send him to sea," was the final conclusion of his mind, after debating the matter for some days, and talking with several friends on the subject. Mr. Howland was generally in earnest when he decided a matter, and but little given to change his purposes. And he was in earnest now. But the moment his intention was announced to his wife, there came from her an unexpected and vigorous opposition.

"No, Andrew," said she, with an emphasis unusual to her in addressing her husband, "that must not be."

"I tell you it must be, Esther," quickly replied Mr. Howland. "Nothing else will save the boy."

"It lacks only that to complete his ruin," said Mrs. Howland, firmly. "Never, Andrew—never will he go on board of a vessel with my consent."

And the mother burst into tears.

"I don't wish to have any contention about this matter, Esther," said Mr. Howland, gravely, as soon as his wife had grown calm, "and I don't mean to have any. But I wish you to understand that I am in earnest. Being fully satisfied that the last hope for Andrew is to send him to sea, I have fully made up my mind to do it. I have already spoken to the captain of a vessel trading to South America.

A few months on ship-board will tame him. He'll be glad enough to behave himself when he gets home."

"I have no faith in this remedy," replied Mrs. Howland, somewhat to the surprise of her husband, who expected to silence her, as usual, with his broadly asserted ultimatum. "Severe remedies have been tried long enough. In my view, a milder course pursued toward the boy would effect more than any other treatment."

"Mildness! Haven't we tried that, over and over again? And hasn't it only encouraged him to bolder acts of disobedience?"

Mrs. Howland sighed. Her mind went back to the past, but none of these instances of mild treatment could she remember. The iron hand had been on him from the beginning, crushing out the good, and hardening the evil into endurance.

"Andrew," said she, after sitting for some time with her eyes upon the floor, speaking in a very calm voice, "he is my son as well as yours—and his welfare is as dear to me as it is to you. As his mother, I am entitled to a voice in all that concerns him; and now, in the sight of heaven, I give my voice distinctly against his being sent to sea."

Mr. Howland seemed startled at this bold speaking in his wife, which, to him, amounted to little less than rebellion against his authority. As the head of the family, it was his prerogative to rule; and he had ruled for years with almost undisputed sway. Not in the least inclined did he feel to give up now, the power which he believed, of right, belonged to him. A sharp retort trembled for a moment on his lips; but he kept back its utterance. He did not, however, waver a single line from his purpose, but rather felt it growing stronger.

No more was said at this time by either. Mrs. Howland sought the earliest opportunity to be alone with her son, when she informed him of his father's purpose to send him to sea. Andrew was somewhat startled by this information, and replied, instantly—

"I don't want to go to sea, mother."

"Nor do I wish you to go, Andrew," said Mrs. Howland. "You are too young to bear the hard usage that would certainly fall to your lot. But your father is very determined about the matter."

"I won't go!" boldly declared the boy.

"Andrew! Andrew! don't speak in that manner," said the mother in a reproving voice.

"I'll run away first!"

An indignant flush came into the lad's face as he said this.

Mrs. Howland was both startled and alarmed at this bold and unexpected declaration, and for a time she hardly knew what to say. At length, in a voice so changed that Andrew looked up, half wonderingly, into her face, she said—

"My son, do you love me?"

Not until the question was repeated did Andrew make any reply. Then he answered, in a low, unsteady voice, for something in her manner had touched his feelings.

"You know I love you, mother; for you are the only one who loves me."

"For the sake, then, of that love, let me ask you to do one thing, Andrew," said Mrs. Howland.

"What is that mother?"

"Go back to your teacher, and ask him to take you into the school again."

A flush came warmly into the boy's face, and he shook his head in a positive manner.

"I wish you to do it for my sake, Andrew," urged Mrs. Howland.

"I can't, mother. And it would not do any good."

"Yes, it will do good. You were wrong in not going punctually to school. All that is now required of you is to acknowledge this, and ask to be restored to your place."

Andrew stood silent and gloomy by his mother's side.

"Were you not wrong in absenting yourself from school at the proper hour?" asked Mrs. Howland, in a calm, penetrating voice.

There was no reply.

"Say, Andrew?" urged the mother.

"Yes, ma'am. I suppose I was."

"Was not your teacher right in objecting to this?"

"I suppose so."

"And right in sending you home if you would not obey the rules of the school?"

The boy assented.

"Very well. Then you alone are to blame for the present trouble, and it rests with you to remove it. For my sake, go back to school, promise to do right in future, and ask to be reinstated. Will not this be better than going to sea, or leaving your father's house, as you thoughtlessly threatened to do just now?"

The tender earnestness with which Mrs. Howland spoke, more than the reasons she urged, subdued the stubborn spirit of the boy.

"You know how determined your father is," she continued. "In his intention to send you to sea he is entirely in earnest, and nothing will prevent his doing so but your going back to school. You threaten to run away. That would avail nothing. You are but a boy, and would be restored to us in a week. Think of the trouble you will bring upon me. Andrew! Andrew! unless you do as I desire, you will break my heart."

Giving way at this point to the pressure on her feelings, Mrs. Howland wept bitterly; and, greatly subdued by his mother's grief, Andrew drew his arm around her neck, and wept with her.

"Go, dear," said Mrs. Howland, as soon as she had recovered herself, parting the hair upon the forehead of her boy, and pressing her lips upon it—"go, and secure your own self-approbation and my happiness, by doing as I desire. Go, now, while your heart beats rightly. Go, and save your mother from untold wretchedness."

And again Mrs. Howland pressed her lips to his forehead. Happily, she prevailed over him. Acting from the good impulses with which she had inspired his better nature, he went to the teacher, who readily consented to take him back into the school on his promise of more orderly conduct in future.

"Andrew has gone back to school," said Mrs. Howland to her husband, on his return home in the evening.

"Gone back to school? I thought the teacher had expelled him."

"Andrew went to him, and promised amendment."

"He did?"

"Yes. After I had talked with him a long time, he consented to do so."

"It is well," briefly, and with much severity in his tone, replied Mr. Howland. He was greatly relieved at this unexpected result; although neither in word or manner did he let his real feelings appear.

CHAPTER VI.

THE thought that came instantly to the mind of Andrew, when his father's resolution to send him to sea was mentioned, was the thought of Emily Winters. For the sake of spending daily a few quickly passing minutes with her, he had subjected himself to reprimand, punishment and disgrace. And his mind instantly reacted against the idea of a separation such as was now threatened. Still he was too proud and stubborn to think for a moment of retracing any of the wrong steps he had made. Nothing but the tender appeal of his mother, whom he did indeed love, amid all his perverseness, could have subdued him. But for the strong attachment felt for Emily, he would have received the intelligence that he was about to be sent to sea, with, pleasure.

For some time after this, Andrew's external conduct was more orderly. But there was so much about him to offend his easily offended father, that he did not escape for even a single day without a frown or harsh word, which soon had the effect to extinguish the few good impulses which the recent subjugation of his will had awakened. He continued to meet Emily on his way to school, but was careful not to linger in her company go long as before. But this pleasure was at length denied him. A person who frequently saw them together, mentioned the fact to Mr. Winters, who immediately reproved his daughter for the association, and positively forbade its continuance. Emily had ever been obedient to her parents in all things, and this command, grievous as it was, she felt bound to obey. On the day after it was given, Andrew lingered for her in vain at the place where they had met daily, until after his school hour. On the next morning he was there earlier than usual, and waited until past his school hour again. But she did not come. Strictly obedient to her parents, she had gone another way so as to avoid the meeting.

During that day, Andrew was absent from school. Having twice missed his gentle friend, he had no heart to enter upon his studies, and so went listlessly wandering about the streets until nearly twelve o'clock. Then he repaired to the neighborhood of her school, and waited to see if she was among the scholars at the time of their dismissal. In a little while the children came pouring forth, and among them his eager eyes soon caught the form of Emily. He was by her side in a moment, saying, as he took her hand—

"Where have you been? I've looked for you these two days."

A crimson flush overspread the face of Emily in an instant, and she gently disengaged the hand he had taken.

Andrew, who, with all his faults, was proud and sensitive, seemed startled by this unexpected reception. For a moment or two he stood gazing upon her downcast face, and then turned from her and walked rapidly away. As he did so, the little girl lifted toward him her gentle eyes, that were now full of tears, and stood gazing after him with a sad expression of countenance until he was out of sight.

"I don't care for anything now!" Such was the ejaculation of Andrew, pausing, and throwing himself, with a reckless air, upon a door-step, so soon as he had passed beyond the view of the friend he had so loved for years, but who now, from some cause unknown to him, had become suddenly estranged. "I don't care for anything now," he repeated. "Let them send me to sea, or anywhere else, if they will! I don't care! I'm not going to school any more! What do I care for school? I do nothing right, any how! It's scold, scold, or flog, flog, all the time! Father says he'll beat goodness into me; but I guess he's beaten it 'amost all out."

With such thoughts passing through his mind, the unhappy boy sat, with his face down, and his head supported on his hands, for some two or three minutes, when he was startled by a well-known voice, whose tones were ever like music to his ears, pronouncing his name.

In an instant he was on his feet. Emily was before him, and her eyes were now fixed upon his face with a sad expression.

"Andrew," said she, "don't be angry. It isn't my fault."

"What isn't your fault?" eagerly inquired the boy, as he grasped her hand.

"Father said I mustn't— "

The little girl hesitated. It seemed as if she couldn't utter the words.

"Said what?"

There was ill-repressed indignation in Andrew's voice.

"Don't be angry! It frightens me when you are angry!" said Emily, looking distressed.

"What did your father say?" asked the boy, in milder tones.

"He said that I mustn't meet you as I went to school any more," replied Emily.

The face of the boy grew crimson, while his lips arched with the angry indignation that swelled in his bosom. He was about giving a passionate vent to his feelings, when he was restrained by the look of distress that overspread the face of his gentle friend, and by the tears that came slowly stealing from her eyes.

"Ain't I as good?"

Thus far Andrew gave utterance to what was in his thoughts, and then, seeing the tears of Emily, checked himself and became silent.

"You ain't angry with me, are you?" asked the little girl, laying her hand upon his, and looking earnestly in his face.

"No; I'm not angry with you, Emily. I'm never angry with you. But it's hard. I'd rather see you than anybody. I don't care what becomes of me now! Let them send me to sea if they will!"

At the word "sea" Emily's face grew pale, and she said in a choking voice,

"O! they won't send you to sea, Andrew?"

"Father threatened to send me to sea if I didn't attend school better."

"But you will attend better, Andrew. I know you will. Oh, it would be dreadful to be sent to sea!"

"I don't know. I'd as lief be there as anywhere else, if I can't see you!"

"But you will see me sometimes. We can't meet any more as we go to school; but we'll see each other often, Andrew."

These words lifted much of the heavy weight that pressed on the feelings of the boy.

"When will we see each other?" he asked.

"I don't know," replied Emily. "Father said we musn't meet going to school; but there will be other chances. Good-by! I wouldn't like father to see me here, for then he would think me a very disobedient girl."

And saying this, Emily turned and ran fleetly away. Andrew's feelings were relieved from the pressure that rested upon them. Still he felt angry and indignant at Mr. Winters, and this state increasing rather than subsiding, tended to encourage other states of mind that were not good. With a feeling of rebellion in his heart he returned home, where he found no difficulty in provoking some reaction, and in falling under the quickly excited displeasure of his father, who was ever more inclined to seek than overlook causes of reproof. The consequence was, that when he left home for school in the afternoon he felt little inclination to attend, and, after a slight debate, yielded to this inclination. A little forbearance and kindness would have softened the child's feelings, and prompted him to enter the right way. But the iron hand was never relaxed, and there was no room beneath it for the crushed heart of the boy to swell with better impulses.

At supper time, on that evening, the boy was absent. He should have been at home nearly two hours before.

"Where is Andrew?" asked Mr. Howland, as they gathered at the table.

"I'm sure I don't know," replied Mrs. Howland, in a voice touched with a deeper concern than usual.

"Has he been home since school was dismissed?"

"No."

"Was there ever such a boy!" exclaimed Mr. Howland.

"Most probably he has been kept in," suggested the mother.

"Edward, go round to the house of his teacher and ask if he was dismissed at five o'clock," said Mr. Howland.

Edward left the table and went on his errand. He soon returned with word that Andrew had not been to school all day.

Knife and fork fell from the hands of Mr. Howland, and the mother's face instantly grew pale.

"I felt troubled about him all day," murmured the latter.

"He was home at dinner time?" said Mr. Howland, as he pushed his chair back from the table.

"Yes."

"Oh dear!—oh dear! What is to become of him? I've tried everything in my power to restrain him from evil, but all is of no avail."

Just at this moment the street-door bell was rung very violently. As each one paused to listen, and the room became perfectly silent, the murmur of many voices could be heard in the street. For a few moments all was breathless expectation. The sound of the servant's feet, as she moved along the passage to the door, throbbed on each heart, and then all sprung from their chairs, as a cry of distress was uttered by the servant, followed by men's voices, and the entrance of a crowd of people.

Poor Mrs. Howland sunk to the floor, nerveless, while Mr. Howland sprung quickly out of the room. The story was soon told. Andrew had been out on the river with some other boys in a boat, from which he had fallen into the water, and was now brought home to his parents, to all appearance, lifeless. It proved in the end that vitality was only suspended; after an hour's unremitted effort, by a skillful physician, the circle of life went on again.

The shock of this event somewhat subdued the mind of Mr. Howland. He felt utterly discouraged about the boy. While in this state of discouragement, he refrained from saying anything to him about his bad conduct. Indeed, in view of this second narrow escape from death, his feelings were a good deal softened toward Andrew, and something like pity took the place of anger. During the two days that the lad was convalescing, his father said little to him; but what little he did say was spoken kindly, and with more of a parental sentiment therein than had been apparent for years. Electrically did this sentiment reach the heart of Andrew. Once when Mr. Howland took his hand, and asked in a kind voice how he felt, tears rushed to his eyes, and his lips quivered so that he could not reply. This was perceived by Mr. Howland, and he felt that his boy was not altogether given over to hardness of heart. In that moment Andrew promised in his own mind, that in future he would be a more obedient boy.

Unhappily, Mr. Howland attributed this subdued and better state of feeling in his son, to the narrow escape from drowning that he had had, and not to the real cause—the change of his own manner toward him. Through the feeble moving of sympathy and kindness in his own heart, there was the beginning of power over the perverse boy, and this power might have been exercised, had the father possessed enough of wisdom and self-denial, until he had gained a complete control over him. But alas! he did not possess this wisdom and self-denial. He was a hard man, and believed in no virtue but that of force. He could drive, but not lead. He could hold with an iron hand, but not restrain by a voice full of the power of kindness.

Before the close of the second day he spoke harshly to Andrew, and did, thereby, such violence to the boy's feelings, that he turned his face from him and wept.

On the third day after the accident Andrew went back to school, and continued, for a time, to go punctually and to attend diligently to his studies. But soon the angry reaction of his father, against little acts of thoughtlessness or disobedience, threw him back into his old state, and he was as bad as ever.

CHAPTER VII.

THUS the struggle went on, Mr. Howland's power to control his boy growing less and less every year. Naturally, considering the relation of the two families of Mr. Howland and Mr. Winters, and the bad reputation of the son of the former, the intercourse between Andrew and Emily was more and more restricted. Still their friendship for each other remained, to a certain extent, undiminished, and they met as often as favorable circumstances would permit. To Emily, the kind feelings entertained for the wayward boy proved sources of frequent unhappiness. Few opportunities for speaking against him were omitted by her parents, and she never heard his name coupled with words of censure without feeling pain. One half that was said of him she did not believe; for she saw more of the bright side of his character than did any one else.

As before intimated, by the time Emily gained her sixteenth year, she had developed so far toward womanhood, that Andrew, who still remained a slender boy in appearance, felt his heart tremble as he looked upon her, and thought of the distance this earlier development had placed between them. And even a greater distance was beginning to exist—the distance that lies between a pure mind and one that is corrupt. As Andrew grew older, he grew worse, and the sphere of his spiritual quality began to be felt, oppressively, at times, by Emily, during the periods of their brief intercourse. Moreover, she was ever hearing some evil thing laid to his charge. At length their intimate intercourse came to an end, and, with the termination of this, was removed the last restraint that held the lad in bounds of external propriety. The cause of this termination we will relate: As Andrew grew older, he grew more and more self-willed, and strayed farther and farther from the right way. Social in his feelings, he sought the companionship of boys of his own age, and by the time he was seventeen, had formed associations of a very dangerous character. Though positively forbidden by his father to be out after night, he disregarded the injunction, and went from home almost every evening. At home there was nothing to attract him; nothing to give him pleasure. A shadow was ever on the brow of his father, and this threw a gloom over the entire household. But, abroad, among his companions, he found a hundred things to interest him. All license tends toward further extremes. It was not long before Andrew found ten o'clock at night too early for him. The theatre was a place positively interdicted by his parents; and, restrained by some lingering respect for his mother's feelings, Andrew had, up to the age of seventeen, resisted the strong desire he felt to see a play. At last, however, he yielded to temptation, and went to the theatre. On returning home about eleven o'clock, he found his father sitting up for him. To the stern interrogation as to where he had been so late, he replied with equivocation, and finally with direct falsehood.

"Andrew," said Mr. Howland, at length, speaking with unusual severity of tone, and with a deliberation and emphasis that indicated a higher degree of earnestness than usual, "if you are out again until after ten o'clock, you remain out all night. To this my mind is fully made up. So act your own good pleasure."

The father and son then separated.

Ten o'clock came on the next night, and Andrew had not returned. For the half hour preceding the stroke of the clock, Mr. Howland had walked the floor uneasily, with his ear harkening anxiously for the sound of the bell that marked his son's return; and, as the time drew nearer and nearer, he half repented the utterance of a law, that, if broken, could not, he feared, but result in injury to the disobedient boy. At last the clock struck ten. He paused and stood listening for over a minute; then he resumed his walk again, and continued his measured paces for over ten minutes longer, intending to give his erring son the benefit of that space of time. But he yielded thus much in his favor in vain. Anger at this deliberate disobedience of a positive order then displaced a portion of anxiety, and he closed, mentally, the door upon his child for that night.

Of his purpose, Mr. Howland said nothing to his wife. He hoped that she would be asleep before Andrew returned, if he returned at all before morning. But in this his hope was not realized. The fact of Andrew's having staid out so late on the night before had troubled her all day, and she had made up her mind to sit up for him now until he came home.

"Come, Esther, it is time to go to bed," said Mr. Howland to his wife, seeing that she made no motion towards retiring.

"You go. I will sit up for Andrew," was replied.

"Andrew can't come in, to-night," said Mr. Howland.

The mother sprung to her feet instantly; her face flushing, and then becoming very pale.

"I told him, last night, that if he staid out again until after ten o'clock, there would be no admission for him until morning. And I shall assuredly keep my word!"

"Oh, Andrew! Don't, don't do this!" pleaded the unhappy mother, in a low, choking voice. "Would you turn an erring son from your door, when danger is hovering around him?"

"He turns himself away. The act is his, not mine," replied Mr. Howland, coldly.

As he spoke, the bell rung.

"There he is, now!" exclaimed the mother, starting toward the door.

"Esther!" Mr. Howland stept in front of his wife, and, looking sternly in her face, added, "Haven't I just said that there was no entrance for him, to-night?"

"But it's early! It's only a few minutes after ten," eagerly replied the mother.

"It's past ten o'clock, and that settles the matter," returned Mr. Howland.

"But where will he go?" asked the mother.

"To the Station House, if he can find no better place. To-morrow he will most probably have a higher appreciation of the comforts of home."

As Mr. Howland closed this sentence, the bell rung again.

"Andrew! I must let him in!" exclaimed the mother, in a tone of anguish, and she made a movement to pass her husband. But a strong hand was instantly laid upon her arm, and a stern voice said—

"Don't interfere with me in this matter, Esther! As the father of that wayward boy, it is my duty to control him."

"This is driving him from his home; not controlling him!"

"I'll bear the responsibility of what I am doing," said Mr. Howland, impatiently. "Why will you interfere with me in this way?"

"Is he not *my* son also?" inquired Mrs. Howland, passing, in her distress of mind, beyond the ordinary spirit of her intercourse with her self-willed husband.

"I am his father," coldly replied the latter, "and knowing my duty toward him, shall certainly do it."

The bell was rung again at this moment, and more loudly than before.

"Oh, Andrew! let me beg of you to open the door!" And Mrs. Howland clasped her hands imploringly, and lifted her eyes running over with tears to her husband's face.

"It cannot be opened to-night, Esther!" was the firm reply. "Have I not said this over and over again. Why will you continue these importunities? They are of no avail."

A loud knocking on the street door was now heard. By this time, a servant who had retired came down from her room and was moving along the passage, when Mr. Howland intercepted her, with the question—

"Where are you going?"

"Some one rung the bell," replied the servant.

"Never mind; go back to your room. You needn't open the door."

"Andrew isn't in yet," said the servant, respectfully.

"Didn't I say, go back to your room?" returned Mr. Howland, in a sharp voice.

Twice more the bell was rung, and twice more the knocking was repeated. Then all remained silent.

"Come, Esther!" said Mr. Howland to his wife, who was sitting on a sofa, with her face buried in her hands. "Let us go up stairs. It is late."

The mother did not stir.

"Esther! did you hear me?"

Slowly, more like a moving automaton than a living creature, did Mrs. Howland arise from her place, and follow her husband up to their chamber. There, without uttering a word, she partially disrobed herself, and getting into bed, buried her tearful face in a pillow. Mr. Howland was soon by her side. Both lay without moving for nearly half an hour, and then the heavy respiration of the husband told that he was asleep. The moment this was apparent, Mrs. Howland, who had lain as still as if locked in deep slumber, crept softly from the bed, and then, with a quick, eager motion, commenced putting on a wrapper. This done, she drew a pair of slippers on her feet, glided noiselessly from the room, and hurried down to the street door, which she softly opened.

The mother had hoped to find her erring son still there. But, as she looked anxiously forth into the darkness, no human form was perceived.

"Andrew!" she called, in a low voice, as she stepped from the door, and threw her eyes up and down the street: "Andrew!"

But all was silent. Descending to the pavement, she passed along a few yards to the steps of the next house, a faint hope in her mind that Andrew might have seated himself there in his disappointment and fallen asleep. But this hope was not realized. Then she passed on to the next house, and the next, with the same purpose and the same result. She was near the corner of the street, when the sound of a closing door fell upon her ear, and the thought that the wind might have shut her own door upon her, filled her with sudden alarm. Running back, she found that what she had feared was too true. She was alone in the street, half-dressed and with her head uncovered, and the door, which closed with a dead-latch, shut against her.

To ring the bell was Mrs. Howland's first impulse. But no one answered to the summons. Every ear was sealed in slumber, and, even were that not the case, no one would come down, unless her husband should awaken, and discover that she was not by his side. Again and again she pulled the bell. But eagerly though she listened, with her ear to the door, not the slightest movement was heard within.

While the mother shrunk close to the door in a listening attitude, the sound of a slow, heavy step was heard approaching along the street. Soon the form of a man came in view, and in a little while he was in front of Mrs. Howland, where he paused, and after standing and looking at her for a few moments, said,

"What's the matter here?"

Mrs. Howland trembled so, that she could make no answer.

The man put his hand on the iron railing, and lifted one foot upon the stone steps leading to the door of the house, saying as he did so,

"Do you live here?"

"Yes!" was replied in a low, frightened voice.

Mrs. Howland now looking at the man more closely, perceived, by his dress, that he was one of the night policemen, and her heart took instant courage.

"Oh," said she, forgetting, for the moment, the unpleasant circumstances by which she was surrounded, and turning to the man as she spoke, "have you seen anything of my son—of Mr. Howland's son—about here to-night?"

"Mrs. Howland! Is it possible!" replied the man, in a respectful voice. Then he added, "I saw him go down the street about half an hour ago."

"Did you! And do you know where he has gone?"

"No, ma'am. He passed on out of sight."

A low moan escaped the mother's lips at this intelligence. A few moments she stood silent, and then placed her hand upon the bell-pull and rung for admittance.

"Is the door locked?" asked the watchman, manifesting surprise.

"No; the wind blew it to, and it has become fastened with the dead-latch."

Both stood silent for some time, but no one answered the bell. The night dews were falling upon the mother's head, and the night air penetrating her thin garments. A shiver ran through her frame, and she felt a constriction of the chest as if she had inhaled sulphur. Again she rung the bell.

"Does no one know of your being out?" asked the watchman.

"All are asleep in the house," replied Mrs. Howland.

At this the watchman came up the steps, and struck two or three heavy blows upon the door with his mace, the sound of which went reverberating through the house, and startling Mr. Howland from his slumber. But not perceiving immediately that his wife was absent from her place by his side, and thinking that his son had renewed his efforts to gain admission, the latter did not make a motion to rise. In a few moments, however, the repeated strokes of the mace, to which was added the loud call of a man in the street below caused him to start up in bed. He then perceived that his wife was not by his side. With an exclamation, he sprang upon the floor, and throwing up the window, called out—

"Who's there?"

"Come down and open the door," was answered by the watchman.

"Who wants to come in?" asked Mr. Howland, his mind beginning by this time to get a little clear from the confusion into which it was at first thrown.

"I do," replied a voice that threw all into bewilderment again.

"Bless me! What does this mean!" exclaimed Mr. Howland, aloud, yet speaking to himself.

"Open the door, quickly," called out Mrs. Howland, in a tone of distress. "Come down and let me in."

Hurriedly Mr. Howland now dressed himself and went down. As he opened the door, his wife glided past him, and ran up stairs. The watchman retired without speaking to the confused and astonished husband, who, recovering his presence of mind, reclosed the door and followed his wife to their chamber.

"Esther! What is the meaning of all this?" asked Mr. Howland, with much severity of manner.

But there was no reply.

"Will you speak?" said he, in a tone of authority.

The home-tyrant had gone a step too far. The meek, patient, long-suffering, much enduring wife, was in no state of mind to bear further encroachments in the direction from which they were now coming. Suddenly she raised herself up from whence she had fallen across the bed, and looking at her husband with an expression that caused him to step back a pace, involuntarily answered.

"By what authority do you speak to me thus?"

"By the authority vested in me as your husband," was promptly answered.

"I was on God's errand, Mr. Howland; searching after the weak, the simple, and the erring! Have you anything to say against the mission? Does your authority reach above His?"

And the mother, lifting her hand, pointed trembling finger upward, while she fixed an eye upon her husband so steady that his own sunk beneath its gaze.

For the space of nearly a minute, the attitude of neither changed, nor was the silence broken. Twice during the time did Mr. Howland lift his eyes to those of his wife, and each time did they fall, after a few moments, under the strange half-defiant look they encountered. At last he said firmly, yet in a more subdued, though rebuking voice,

"This to me, Esther?"

"Am I not a mother?" was asked in response to this, yet without a perceptible tremor in her voice.

"You are a wife, as well as a mother," replied Mr. Howland, "and, as a wife, are under a sacred obligation to regard the authority committed to your husband by God."

"Have I not just said to you," returned Mrs. Howland, "that I was on God's errand? Does your authority go beyond His?"

"When did He speak to you?" There was a covert sneer in the tone with which this half impious interrogation was made.

"I heard his still, small voice in my mother's heart," replied Mrs. Howland, meekly, "and I went forth obedient thereto, to seek the straying child you had so harshly and erringly turned from your door: thus does God shut the door of Heaven against no wandering one who comes to it and knocks for entrance."

"Esther! I will not hear such language from your lips!" There was an unsteadiness in the voice of Mr. Howland, that marked the effect his wife's unexpected and searching words had produced.

"Then do not seek to stand between me and my duty as a mother," was her firm reply. "Too long, already, have you placed yourself between me and this duty. But that time is past."

As Mrs. Howland uttered these words, she passed across the room to a window, which she threw up, and leaning her body out, looked earnestly up and down the street. For a reaction like this Mr. Howland was not prepared. He was, in fact, utterly confounded. Had there been the smallest sign of irresolution on the part of his wife—the nearest appearance of weakness in the will so suddenly opposed to his own—he would have known what to do. But nothing of this was apparent, and he hesitated about advancing again to the contest, while there was so strong a doubt as to the issue.

For a long time Mr. Howland moved about the room, while his wife continued to sit, listening, at the window.

"Come, Esther," said the former, at length, in a voice greatly changed from its tone when he last spoke. "You had better retire. It is useless to remain there. Besides, you are in danger of taking cold. The air is damp and chilly."

"You can retire—I shall sleep none, to-night," was answered to this. And then Mrs. Howland looked again from the window. "Where—where can he have gone?" she said aloud, though speaking to herself. "My poor, unhappy boy!"

Mr. Howland made no answer to this. He had no satisfying intelligence to offer, nor any words of comfort that it would be of avail to speak.

Thus the greater portion of that long remembered night was passed—Mrs. Howland sitting at the window, vainly waiting and watching for her son, and Mr. Howland walking the floor of the room, his mind given up to troubled and rebuking thoughts. In his hardness and self-will he had justified himself up to this in his course of conduct pursued toward his children; but he was in doubt now. A question as to whether he had been right or not had come into his mind, and disturbed him to the very centre.

CHAPTER VIII.

WHEN Mr. Howland threatened his son with exclusion from the house, if he were away at ten o'clock, Andrew's feelings were in a state of reaction against his father, and he said to himself, in a rebellious spirit—

"We'll see if you will."

But after growing cooler, he came into a better state of mind; and, in view of consequences such as he knew would be visited on him, decided not to come in contact with his father in this particular—at least not for the present. If turned from his own door at midnight, where was he to find shelter? This question he could not answer to his own satisfaction.

After supper, on the evening succeeding that in which he had visited the theatre, Andrew left home and went to an engine-house in the neighborhood, where he joined about a dozen lads and young men as idle and aimless as himself. With these he spent an hour or two, entering into their vicious and debasing conversation, when a person with whom he had gone to see the play on the previous evening, proposed to him to go around to the theatre again. Andrew objected that he had no money, but the other said that he could easily procure checks, and volunteered to ask for them. Still Andrew, whose thoughts were on the passing time, refused to go. He meant to be home before the clock struck ten.

"Come round with me, then," urged the lad.

"What time is it?" asked Andrew.

"Only a little after nine o'clock," was replied.

"Are you certain?"

"Oh, yes. I heard the clock strike a short time ago. It isn't more than a quarter past nine."

"I thought it was later than that."

"No. It's early yet; so, come along. I want to talk to you."

Thus urged, Andrew went with the boy. The theatre was some distance away. Just as they reached it, a clock was heard to strike.

"Bless me!" exclaimed Andrew. "Three—four—five—six—seven—eight—nine—TEN!" And, as he uttered the last word, he started back the way he had come, running at full speed. It was ten o'clock—the hour he was required to be at home, under penalty of having the door closed against him. How troubled he felt! How strongly his heart beat! He had not intended to disregard his father's command in this instance. In fact, during the day, he had reflected more than usual, and many good resolutions had formed themselves in his mind.

"I wish I could be better," he said to himself involuntarily, a great many times. And then he would sigh as he thought of the difficulties that were in his way. At dinner time he came to the table with his feelings a good deal subdued. But it so happened, that, during the morning, Mr. Howland had heard of some impropriety of which he had been guilty a month previous, and felt called upon to reprimand him, therefore, with considerable harshness. The consequence was, that the boy left the table without finishing his dinner, at which his father became very much incensed. The angry feelings of the latter had not subsided when tea-time came, and he met the family at their evening meal with the clouded face he too often wore. The supper hour passed in silence. After leaving the table, Andrew, to whom the sphere of the house was really oppressive, from its entire want of cheerfulness and mutual good feeling, went out to seek the companionship of those who were more congenial.

"There's nothing pleasant here," he said, as he stood in the door, half disposed to leave the house. "If there only was! But I won't think of it!" he added with impulsive quickness; and, as he murmured these words, he descended the steps to the street, and walked slowly away.

Thus, it will be seen, the wayward boy was virtually driven out by the harshness and want of sympathy which prevailed at home, to seek the society of those who presented a more attractive exterior, but who were walking in the paths of evil, and whose steps tended to destruction.

But, though thus thrust out, as it were, from the circle of safety, Andrew still preserved his intention of being at home at the hour beyond which his father had warned him not to be away. It has been seen how, through an error as to time, he was betrayed into unintentional transgression. Not an instant did he pause on his return from the theatre, but ran all the way homeward at a rapid speed. Arriving at the door, he pulled the bell, and then stood panting from excitement. For a short time he waited, in trembling anxiety, but no one answered his summons. Then he rung the bell more violently than before. Still none came to let him in, and his heart began to fail him.

"Surely father don't mean to keep me out!" said he to himself. "He wouldn't do that. Where am I to go for shelter at this hour?"

And again he pulled the bell, causing it to ring longer and louder than before. Then he leaned close to the door and listened, but no sound reached his ears. Growing impatient, he next tried knocking. All his efforts to gain admission, however, proved unavailing; and ceasing at last to ring or knock, he sat down upon the stone steps, and covering his face with his hands, wept bitterly. For over a quarter of an hour he remained seated at the threshold of his father's house, from which he had been excluded. During that period, much of his previous life passed in review before him, and the conclusions of the boy's mind were at last expressed in these words—

"I believe father hates the very sight of me! He says I'm going to ruin, and so I am; but he is driving me there. What does he think I'm going to do, to-night? If he cared for me, would he let me sleep in the streets? I have tried to do right, but it was of no use. When I tried the hardest, he was the crossest, and made me do wrong whether I would or not. I don't care what becomes of me now!"

As Andrew uttered these last words, a reckless spirit seized him, and starting up, he walked away with a firm step. But he had gone only a block or two, before his mind again became oppressed with a sense of his houseless condition, and pausing, he murmured, in a sad under tone—

"Where shall I go?"

For a little while he stood irresolute, and then moved on again. For several squares farther he walked, with no definite purpose in his mind, when he came to a row of three or four unfinished houses, the door of one of which was partially opened; at least so much so, that it was only necessary to pull off a narrow strip of board in order to effect an entrance. With the sight of these houses came the suggestion to the mind of Andrew that he might find a place to sleep therein for the night, and acting upon this, he passed up the plank leading to the door least securely fastened, and soon succeeded in getting it open. But, just as he stepped within, a heavy hand was laid upon him from behind, and a rough voice said—

"What are you doing here, sir?"

Turning, Andrew found himself in the custody of a policeman.

For a few moments every power of mind and body forsook the unhappy boy, and he stood shrinking and stammering before the officer—thus confirming a suspicion of intended incendiarism in the mind of that functionary.

"Come! you must go with me." And the officer commenced moving down the plank that connected the door with the ground, drawing Andrew after him.

"I was only going to sleep there," said the frightened boy, as soon as the power of speech had returned.

"Of course," returned the policeman, "I understand all that. But I'll find a better place in which you can spend the night. So come along with me."

Remonstrance on the part of Andrew was all in vain, and so, watching an opportunity, he made an effort to escape. But he ran only a few yards before he was tripped up by the officer, when falling, he struck his forehead on the curb-stone, wounding it severely.

"Look here!" said the officer, in a resolute voice, passing his heavy mace before the eyes of Andrew; "if you try this again I'll knock you senseless!"

Then grasping his arm more firmly, he added—

"Move along quickly!"

With his head aching severely from the fall, and the blood trickling down his face from the wound on his forehead, Andrew walked along by the side of the officer, who continued to keep hold of him. In passing under a gas-lamp, they met a lady and gentleman. The former Andrew recognized at a glance, and she knew him, even with his bloody face, and uttered a cry of surprise and alarm. It was Emily Winters returning with her father from the house of a friend, where they had stayed to an unusually late hour. The officer was about pausing, but Andrew sprung forward, saying as he did so, in an under tone—

"Don't stop!"

At the same instant Mr. Winters urged on his daughter, and the parties were separated in a moment.

"Unhappy boy!" said the father of Emily, who had also recognized Andrew, "his folly and evil are meeting a just but severe return. His poor mother!—when she hears of this it will almost break her heart. What an affliction to have such a son!"

"Did you see the blood on his face?" asked Emily, in a choking voice, while her hand shook so violently, as it rested on the arm of, her father, that he felt the tremor in every nerve.

"I did," he replied.

"What was the matter? He must be badly hurt. What could have done it?"

"He's been quarreling with some one, I presume," coldly replied Mr. Winters, who did not like the interest his daughter manifested.

Emily made no reply to this, and they walked the rest of the way home in silence.

CHAPTER IX.

IT was within an hour of daylight when Mrs. Howland, worn down by her long vigil, fell asleep, and an hour after the sun had risen, before her troubled slumber was broken. Then starting up, she eagerly inquired of her husband, who had already arisen, and was walking about the room, if Andrew had yet returned. Mr. Howland merely shook his head.

Soon after, breakfast was announced, and the family assembled at the table; but one place was vacant.

"Where is Andrew?" asked Mary.

No answer was made to this question; and Mary saw by the expression of her parents faces, that to repeat it would not be agreeable. A few moments afterward the bell rung. As the steps of a servant were heard moving along the passage toward the door, Mr. and Mrs. Howland sat listening in breathless expectation. Soon the servant came down, and said that a man wished to see Mr. Howland.

At these words the latter started up from the table and left the room. At the street door he found a man, whose appearance indicated his attachment to the police of the city.

"Mr. Howland!" said he, respectfully, yet with the air of a man who had something not very agreeable to communicate.

"That is my name," replied Mr. Howland, striving, but in vain, to assume an air of unconcern.

"You are wanted at the Mayor's office," said the policeman.

"For what purpose?" was inquired.

"Your son is before his Honor, on a charge of attempting to set fire to a row of new buildings last night."

At this intelligence, Mr. Howland uttered an exclamation of distress, and stepping back a pace or two, leaned heavily against the wall.

"Well! What is wanted with me?" asked the unhappy father, recovering himself, after a few moments.

"To go his bail," replied the officer. "The Mayor demands a thousand dollars bail, in default of which, he will have to go to prison and there await his trial."

"Let him go to prison!" said Mr. Howland, in a severe tone of voice. He was beginning to regain his self-possession.

"No, Andrew!" came firmly from the lips of Mrs. Howland, who had followed her husband, unperceived, to the door, and who had heard the dreadful charge preferred against her son. "Don't say that! Go and save him from the disgrace and wrong that now hang over his head—and go quickly!"

"Yes, Mr. Howland," said the officer, "your lady is right. You should not let him go to prison. That will do him no good. And, moreover, he may be innocent of the crime laid to his charge."

"He must be innocent. My boy has many faults, but he would not be guilty of a crime like this," said Mrs. Howland. "Oh, Mr. Howland! go! go quickly and save him from these dreadful consequences. If you do not, I must fly to him. They shall not imprison my poor boy!"

"This is folly, Esther!" returned Mr. Howland, severely. "He has got himself, by his bad conduct, into the hands of the law, and it will do him good to feel its iron grip. I am clear for letting him at least go to prison, and remain there for a few days. By that time he will be sick enough of his folly."

"I would not advise this," suggested the officer. "Depend upon it, if his present position is of no avail toward working change for the better—sending him to prison will harden, rather than reform him."

"Andrew!" said Mrs. Howland, with a firmness and decision of tone that marked a high degree of resolution on her part—"if you do not go his bail, I will find some person who will."

"Esther!" The offended husband fixed a look of stern rebuke upon his wife; but her large eyes looked steadily into his, and he saw in them, not rebellion, or anger—but a spirit that his own heart told him instinctively, it would be folly for him to oppose. That look determined his action.

"I'll go with you," said he, after pausing a few moments, turning to the officer as he spoke.

The charge brought against Andrew by the watchman, was an intention to set fire to the buildings in which he found him. Several unfinished houses had been burned of late, and there was some excitement in the public mind thereat. Had it not been for this, Andrew might have made his way into the building where he intended to sleep, without, in all probability, attracting attention. Unfortunately for him, a few matches were found in one of his pockets. This fact, added to his attempt to escape, and the rather exaggerated statement of the watchman, caused the Mayor to look upon the case as one that ought to go before the Court. He accordingly decided to require an appearance, under bail.

Not a word was spoken to Andrew by his stern father, on the arrival of the latter at the Mayor's office. Mr. Howland looked at the evidence which went to support the charge of intended incendiarism against his son, and to his mind, prejudiced as it was against that son, the evidence was conclusive. In fact, the watchman's eyes had seen rather more, than in reality, was to be seen, and his testimony was strongly colored.

The required security given, Mr. Howland, without turning toward his son, or speaking to him, left the office.

"You can go home, young man," said the Mayor, addressing Andrew.

"Oh, sir!" exclaimed the unhappy boy, in a distressed tone—"I am not guilty of this thing. Father turned me from the door because I was not at home at ten o'clock, and I had no place to sleep."

"Disobedience to parents ever brings trouble," replied the Mayor, in a voice of admonition. "Go home, and try to behave better in future. If innocent, you will no doubt be able to make it so appear when your trial comes on before the Court."

Slowly the lad arose, and with a troubled and downcast look, retired from the office.

"Where is Andrew?" eagerly asked the mother, as Mr. Howland entered the house, after returning from the errand upon which he had gone.

"I left him at the Mayor's office," was coldly replied.

"Did you go his bail?"

"Yes."

"Why didn't he come home with you?"

"I didn't ask him."

"Andrew!"

Mr. Howland started at the tone of voice with which his name was pronounced. Again there was an expression in the eyes of his wife that subdued him.

"I gave bail for his appearance at Court, and then came away. He will, no doubt, be home in a few minutes," he replied. "But I do not wish to hold any intercourse with him; for he has disgraced both himself and me."

"Is he not your son?" asked the mother, solemnly.

"He is not a son worthy of affection and regard."

"Andrew! when the sons of men wandered far away from God, and broke all his laws, did He turn from them as you have turned from this erring boy? No! All day long He stretched forth His hands to them, and said, in a voice full of infinite kindness, 'Return unto Me; why will you die?' It is not Godlike to be angry at those who sin against us; but Godlike to draw them back with cords of love from error. Oh, Andrew! you have wronged this boy!"

"Esther! I will not hear the utterance of such language from any one!" exclaimed Mr. Howland, whose imperious nature could ill brook an accusation like this.

"I have uttered only what I believe to be true," answered the wife, in a milder tone, yet with a firmness that showed her spirit to be unsubdued. No further words passed between them. Half an hour afterward, up to which time Andrew had not come home, Mr. Howland left the house and went to his place of business.

Time passed on until nearly noon, and yet Andrew was still away. Mrs. Howland, whose mind was in a state of strong excitement, could bear her suspense and fear no longer, and she resolved to go out and seek for her wandering son. She had dressed herself, and was just taking up her bonnet, as the door of her room opened, and Andrew came in, looking pale and distressed. Across his forehead was a deep, red mark, the scar left by the wound he received, when he fell on the pavement, in the attempt to escape from the watchman.

"My son!" exclaimed Mrs. Howland, in a voice that thrilled the poor boy's heart—for it was full of sympathy and tenderness—and then she threw her arms around his neck and kissed him.

Overcome by this reception, Andrew wept aloud. As soon as he could speak, he said—

"Indeed, indeed, mother! I am innocent. You wouldn't let me in last night, and I was going to sleep in the building, when the watchman came and said I meant to set it on fire! I'm bad enough, mother, but not so wicked as that! Why should I set a house on fire?"

"I didn't believe it for a moment, Andrew," replied Mrs. Howland. "But, oh! isn't it dreadful?"

"I'm not to blame, mother," said the weeping boy. "I didn't mean to stay out later than ten. But I was deceived in the time. I was a good way off when the clock struck, and I ran home as fast as I could. I'm sure it wasn't ten minutes after when I rang the bell. But nobody would let me in; not even *you*, mother—and I thought so hard of *that!*"

With what a pang did these last words go through the heart of Mrs. Howland.

"I wanted to let you in," replied the mother, "but your father said that I must not do so."

"And so you left me to sleep in the streets," said the boy, with much bitterness. "I couldn't have turned a dog off in that way!"

"Don't, don't speak so, Andrew! You will break my heart!" returned the mother, sobbing, "I did open the door for you, but you were not there."

"I knocked and rung a good while."

"I know. But I had to wait until your father was asleep. Then I went down, but it was too late."

"Yes—yes, it was too late," said Andrew, speaking now in a firmer voice. "And it is too late now. I am to be tried as a felon, and it may be, will be sent to the State Prison. Oh, dear!"

And he covered his face with his hands, and sobbed.

What little comfort she had to offer her unhappy child, was offered by Mrs. Howland. But few rays of light came through the heavy clouds that enveloped both of their hearts.

At dinner time, Andrew declined meeting his father at the table.

"Go and tell him," said the unyielding man, when the servant, who had been sent to his room to call him to dinner, came back and said that he did not wish to come down, "that he cannot have a mouthful to eat unless he comes to the table."

"No, no, Andrew—don't say that!" quickly spoke Mrs. Howland.

"I do say it, and I mean it," replied Mr. Howland, fixing his eyes rebukingly upon his wife.

Mrs. Howland answered nothing. But her purpose to stand between her unrelenting husband and wandering son, was none the less fixed; and in her countenance Mr. Howland read this distinctly. Accordingly, so soon as the latter had left the house, she took food to Andrew, who still remained in his room, at the same time that she expressed to him her earnest wish that he would meet the family at the tea-table in the evening.

"I don't want to meet father," he replied to this. "He will only frown upon me."

"He is, of course, very much fretted at this occurrence," said the mother. "And you cannot much wonder at it, Andrew."

"He is more to blame than I am," was answered in an indignant tone.

"Don't speak of your father in that way, my son," said the mother, a gentle reproof in her voice.

"I speak as I feel, mother. Is it not so?"

An argument on this subject Mrs. Howland would not hold with her boy, and she therefore changed it; but she did not cease her appeals to both his reason and his feelings, until he yielded to her wishes. At supper time he joined the family at table—it was his first meeting with his father since morning. Oh, what an intense desire did he feel for a kind reception from his stern parent! It seemed to him that such a reception would soften everything harsh and rebellious, and cause him to throw himself at his feet, and make the humblest confessions of error, and the most truthful promise of future well doing. Alas! for the repentant boy! no such reception awaited him. His father did not so much as turn his eyes upon his son, and, during the meal, maintained a frigid silence. Andrew ate but a few mouthfuls. He had no appetite for food. On leaving the table, he went into one of the parlors, whither he was followed in a little while, by his younger brother, Edward, who was, by nature, almost as hard and unsympathsizing as his father. It was the first time, on that day, that the two boys had been alone.

"Set a house on fire!" said Edward, in a half-sneering, half-censorious, tantalizing voice.

"If you say that again, I'll knock you down!" fell sharply from the lips of Andrew, in whom his father's repulsive coldness was beginning to awaken bad feelings.

"Set a house on fire!" repeated Edward, in a tone still more aggravating.

The words had scarcely left his tongue, ere the open hand of his brother came along side of his head, with a force that knocked him across the room. At this instant Mr. Howland entered. He made no inquiry as to the cause of the blow he saw struck, but took it for granted that it was an unprovoked assault of Andrew upon his brother. Yielding to the impulse of the moment, he caught the former by the arm, in a fierce grip, and struck him with his open hand, as he had struck his brother, repeating the blow three or four times.

Andrew neither shrunk from the blows, cried out, nor offered the smallest resistance, but stood firmly, until his incensed father had satisfied his outraged feelings.

"You forgot, I suppose, that I could strike also?" said the latter angrily, when he released his son from the tight grasp, with which he held him.

"No sir," replied Andrew, with a calmness that surprized, yet still more incensed his father; "I thought nothing about it. I punished Edward as he deserved; and if he says to me what he did just now, will repeat the punishment, if it cost me my life."

"Silence!" cried Mr. Howland.

"I said nothing but the truth," spoke up Edward.

"What did you say?" inquired the father.

"I told him that he'd set a house on fire."

"And lied when he said it," calmly and deliberately spoke Andrew.

"Silence! I'll have no such language in my presence!" angrily retorted Mr. Howland.

"It is bad enough to be accused falsely by a lying policeman," said Andrew, "but to have the charge repeated by my own brother is more than I can or will bear. And I warn Edward, in your presence, not to try the experiment again. If he does he will not escape so lightly."

"Silence, I say!"

Andrew remained silent.

"Edward, leave the room," said Mr. Howland. There was little sternness in his voice, as he thus spoke to his favorite boy.

The lad retired. For several minutes Mr. Howland walked the floor, and Andrew who had seated himself, waited in a calm, defiant spirit, for him to renew the interview. It was at length done in these words—

"What do you expect is to become of you, sir?"

Not feeling inclined to answer such an interrogation, Andrew continued silent.

"Say!" repeated the father, "what do you think is to become of you?"

Still the boy answered not a word.

"Under bail to answer for a crime— "

"Which I never committed—nor designed to commit!" spoke up Andrew, quickly interrupting his father, and fixing his eyes upon, him with an unflinching gaze.

"It is easy to make a denial. But the evidence against you is positive."

"The evidence against me is a positive lie!" was Andrew's indignant response.

"I won't be talked to in this way!" said Mr. Howland, in an offended tone. "No son of mine shall insult me!"

"A strange insult to a father, for a son to declare himself innocent of a crime falsely laid to his charge," replied Andrew, with a strong rebuke in his voice. "A true father would be glad— "

"Silence!" again fell harshly from the lips of Mr. Howland. "Silence, I say; I will hear no such language from a son of mine!"

Without a word, Andrew arose, and, retiring from the room, took up his hat and left the house—the relation between him and his father by no means in a better position than it was before. Within a few minutes of ten o'clock the boy returned, and, being admitted, went up to his room without joining the family.

On the next morning, one or two of the daily papers contained an account of Andrew's arrest, with his father's name and all the particulars of the transaction. Any one reading this account, with the reporter's comment, could not help but believe that Andrew was a desperate bad boy, and undoubtedly guilty in design of incendiarism.

"See what a disgrace you have brought upon us!" exclaimed Mr. Howland, flinging a paper, containing this mortifying intelligence in the face of his son.

The boy took up the paper, and read the paragraph referred to with a burning cheek. He made no remark, but sat for some time in a state of profound abstraction. No one guessed the thoughts that were passing through his mind, nor the utter hopelessness that was lying, with a heavy weight, upon his spirit. Before him was the image of Emily. She had seen him with his blood-disfigured face, in the hands of the watchman; and now she would see this slanderous story, and what was worse, believe it!

Some two hours subsequently, while walking along the street, Andrew perceived Emily, within a few paces of him. He looked her steadily in the face, and saw that she saw him; for a quick flush overspread her countenance. But, averting her eyes, she passed him without a further sign of recognition.

At night-fall, the boy did not return to his home.

Anxiously did the time pass with Mrs. Howland until ten o'clock, and yet he was away. Eleven—twelve—one o'clock, pealed on the ear of the watching mother, but he came not. It was all in vain that her husband remonstrated with her. His words passed her unheeded; and she remained waiting and watching, until near the hour of morning, but her waiting and watching were all in vain.

Two days passed—yet there came no tidings of the absent boy. On the third day, Mrs. Howland received the following letter:—

> "MY DEAR MOTHER:—I have left my home—forever! What is to become of me, I do not know. But I can remain with you no longer. Father treats me like a dog—or worse than a dog;

and he has never treated me much better. I have tried to do right a great many times; but it was of no use. The harder I tried to do right, the more he found fault with me. He was always blaming me for something I didn't do. It is all a lie of the watchman's about my setting the house on fire. Such a thing never entered my mind. Father wouldn't let me in, and I had to sleep somewhere. He wouldn't speak a word for me in the Mayor's office. So it's all his fault that I am to be tried before the Court. But I'm not going to be sent to the Penitentiary. Father is my bail for a thousand dollars. I shall be sorry if he has to pay it; but it will be better for him to do that, than for me to go to the Penitentiary for nothing. So, good-by, mother, I love you! You have always been good to me. If father had been as good, I would have been a better boy. Don't grieve about me. It's better that I should leave home. You'll all be happier. If I ever return to you, I will be different from what I am now. Farewell mother! Don't forget me. I will never forget you. Don't grieve about me. The thought of that troubles me the most. But it is better for me to go away, mother—better for us all. Farewell.

"ANDREW."

CHAPTER X.

A YEAR elapsed before any tidings of the wanderer came. Then Mrs. Howland received a few lines from him, dated in a Southern city, where he spoke of having just arrived from South America. He had little to say of himself, beyond that he was well; and did not speak of visiting home.

After reading this letter, Mrs. Howland placed it in the hands of her husband, who read it also, and then gave it back without a remark. He checked an involuntary sigh as he did so. Not the slightest reference was made to him by his son; a fact that he did not overlook, and that he did not observe without a sense of disappointment. The long absence of his wayward boy had softened his feelings toward him; and with pain he remembered many acts of harshness that now seemed to have in them too much of the element of severity. At the term of the Court, which was held soon after Andrew went away, the Grand Jury failed to obtain sufficient evidence to justify the finding of a bill against him, and released the security given for his appearance at Court. This fact, with a previous questioning of the policeman by whom Andrew had been arrested, satisfied Mr. Howland that the boy had been unjustly suspected of an intention to commit a crime. But this conviction had come too late. The effects of that unjust accusation had already fallen in sad consequences upon the head of the poor boy; and the father could not force from his mind the painful conviction that he was, mainly, responsible for these consequences.

Another year went by, but during all the time, no further tidings came of Andrew. To his first letter, Mrs. Howland had immediately replied, urging him, by every tender consideration, to return to his home. But she had no means of knowing whether it had ever been received. Upon her the effect of his absence had been, for a time, of the most serious character. For a few weeks after he went away, both body and mind were prostrated; to this succeeded a state of mental depression, which continued so long that her friends began to fear for her reason. Not until after the lapse of a year, when she received the above-mentioned letter from her son, did her mind attain to anything like its former state. The knowledge that he was yet, alive, that he thought of her, and still cherished her memory, gave a new impulse to her fainting spirit, and a quicker motion to the circle of life. There was yet room to hope for him. But, as time went on, there came not back even a faint echo to the voice she had sent after him, her heart failed her again. Yet time, which imparts strength to all in trouble, had done its work for her also. The care and labor that ever attend the mother's position among her children, had bent her thoughts so much away from Andrew, that, while his absence left a constant weight upon her feelings, it did not crush them down as before, into a waveless depression.

The second year of Andrew's absence came to a close; but nothing further was heard from him. And it was the same with the third, fourth, and fifth years. In the meantime, there had been many changes in Mr. Howland's family. Mary had married against her father's wishes, and both herself and husband had been so unkindly treated by him on the occasion and afterward, that neither of them visited at his house.

Henry Markland, the husband of Mary, had been rather a gay young man, and this, with some other things which had come to his ears, created a prejudice in the mind of Mr. Howland against him. As to what was good in Markland, and likely to overbalance defects, he did not inquire. The hue of his prejudice colored everything. Men like Mr. Howland, who seek to bend everything into forms suited to their own narrow range of ideas, are rarely successful in attaining their ends. The principle of freedom is too deeply interwoven with all the tissues of the human mind to admit of this. From earliest infancy there is a reaction against arbitrary power; and, those who are wise, have long since discovered that it is a much easier task to lead than force the young into right ways. Those who would truly govern children, must first learn to govern themselves. Let a parent break his own imperious will before he tries to break the will of his child; and he will be far more successful in the work he essays. to perform. But not so had Mr. Howland learned his duty in life. Without being, aware of the fact, he was a domestic tyrant, and sought to establish a family despotism. And the worst of the whole was, he did nearly all this work in the name of religion! Not that he was a hypocrite. No; Mr. Howland was sincere in his professions of piety. But he was a narrow-minded man, and did much in the name of religion, that in no way harmonized with its true character. His faith was a blind faith, and he sacrificed to the god of his imagination in the unyielding spirit of a dehumanizing superstition. Of necessity, he marred everything upon which he sought to impress the form of his own mind.

Erroneous judgment of others is almost certain to mark the conclusions of such a man's mind; and it is no wonder that Mr. Howland erred in his conclusions respecting the true character of his daughter's husband, who had in him many good qualities, and was sincerely attached to Mary. The great defect appertaining to him, was the fact that he was not a church member. Mr. Howland did not look past the veil of a profession, to see if there was in the ground work of the young man's character a basis of right principles—the only true foundation upon which a religious structure can be built.

Because he did not belong to the church, and make an open profession, he classed him with the irreligious, and considered him as one whose feet were moving swiftly along the road to destruction.

And so, instead of wisely seeking to win the confidence of the young man, that he might gain an influence over him for good, Mr. Howland, offended because his daughter could not obey him in a matter so vital to her happiness, angrily repulsed and insulted both of them, even after he saw that a marriage was inevitable. The consequence was, as has been mentioned, that Markland, who possessed an independent spirit, would not go to the house of his father-in-law; and Mary, resenting the wanton attacks that had been made upon her husband's feelings in more than one or two instances, absented herself also. Mr. Howland, however much he might regret the hardness of his unavailing opposition, was not the man to yield anything; and so the breach remained open, in spite of all the grieving mother's efforts to heal it.

Of all his children, Mr. Howland saw most to hope for in Edward, who early perceived it to be his best policy to humor his father, and, by that means, gain the ends he had in view. Cold in his temperament, he was generally able to control himself in a way to deceive his father as to the real motives that were in his heart. Thus, while Mr. Howland, by his peculiar treatment of his children, drove some of them off, he made this one a hypocrite.

Not the smallest affection existed between Edward and the other children, who knew too well the selfish and evil qualities that lay concealed beneath an external of propriety, put on especially for his father's eyes. The mother, too, saw beneath the false exterior assumed by her son, who treated her, except when his father was present, with little respect or affection.

Martha, the youngest, was a sweet tempered girl, who had managed to keep, as a general thing, beyond the sphere of antagonism that marked the intercourse of the other children. To her mother, as she grew up, she proved a source of comfort; and she could, at almost any time, dispel by her smiles the cloud that too often rested on the brow of her morose father.

On reaching his seventeenth year, Edward had been placed in a store by his father, for the purpose of acquiring knowledge of mercantile affairs. A young man in this position, if he has any ambition to make his way in the world, soon gets his mind pretty well filled with money-making ideas, and sees the way to wealth opening in a broad vista before him. Every day he hears about this, that, and the other one, who started in business but a few years before, with little or no capital, and who are now worth their tens of thousands; and he thus learns to aspire after wealth, without being made to feel sensibly the fact, that the number who grow rich rapidly are as one to a hundred compared with those who succeed as the result of small beginnings united with long continued and untiring application. Long before Edward reached his twenty-first year, he had so fully imbibed the spirit of the atmosphere in which he breathed, that his mind was made up to go into business for himself as soon as he attained his majority. This idea Mr. Howland sought to discourage in his son; but Edward never gave it up. Soon after he was twenty-one, an offer to go into a business, that promised a large return was made, provided a few thousand dollars capital could be furnished. Not a moment did Edward rest until he had prevailed upon his father, ever too ready to yield a weak compliance to the wishes of this son, to place in his hands the amount of money required. To do this, was, at the time, no easy matter for Mr. Howland, whose own business was far from being as good as usual and whose pecuniary affairs were not in the most easy condition. Six thousand dollars was the amount of capital he was obliged to raise, and it was not accomplished without considerable sacrifice.

Edward and his partner were what are usually called "enterprising young men," and they drove ahead in the business they had undertaken at a kind of railroad speed, calculating their profits at an exceedingly high range. It is not surprising that, by the end of the first year, they required a little more capital to help them through with their engagements, the furnishing of which fell upon Mr. Howland; who, in this emergency, passed his notes to the new firm for several thousand dollars.

It is not our purpose to trace, step by step, the progress of this young man in the work of ruining his father and disgracing himself by dishonest practices in business. Enough, that in the course of three years, the "enterprising young men," who made from the beginning such rapid strides toward fortune, found their course suddenly checked, and themselves involved in hopeless bankruptcy. But, with themselves rested not the evil consequences of failure; others were included in the disaster, and among them Mr. Howland, who was so badly crippled as to be obliged to call his creditors together, and solicit a reduction and extension of the claims they had against him. To Mr. Howland, this was a crushing blow. He was not only a man who strictly regarded honesty in his dealings, but he was proud of his honesty, and in his pride, had often been harsh in his judgment of others when in circumstances similar to those in which he was now placed. To be forced to ask of his creditors both a reduction and an extension, humiliated him to a degree, that for a time, almost deprived him of the power of doing business. From that time, there was a perceptible change in the man of iron. His tall, erect form seemed to shrink downward; his head bent toward his bosom, and the harsh lines on his brow and around his less tightly closed lips grew softer. His indignation against Edward was so great, when he finally comprehended the character of the transactions in which he had been engaged, involving as they did a total absence of integrity, that he turned his back upon him angrily, saying, as he did so—

"Never come into my presence again, until you come an honest man!"

On the day after this utterance of the father's indignant feelings, Edward left the city; and it was the opinion of many that he went with a pocket full of money. They were not far wrong.

Thus, of all his children, only the youngest remained with Mr. Howland. All the rest were estranged from him; and in spite of all his efforts to push the conviction from his mind, he could not help feeling that he was to blame for the estrangement.

CHAPTER XI.

NEARLY eight years from the time Andrew Howland left his home have passed, and we now bring him before the reader as a discharged United States' dragoon, having just concluded a five years' service in the far West. He had enlisted, rather than steal, at a time when he found it impossible to obtain employment, and had gone through the hard and humiliating service of a trooper on our extreme frontier, under an assumed name, omitting to write home during the entire period, lest by any chance a knowledge of his position might be communicated to his mother, and (her memory had never faded) to Emily Winters. The images of these two, the only ones he loved in the world, were green in his bosom. They were drawing him homeward with a force of attraction that grew stronger and stronger as the end of his service approached. Nearly three years had elapsed since he had met any one recently from the East who was able to answer, satisfactorily, the few inquiries he ventured to make; and now he was all impatience to return.

Steadily, for a long time, had the young man looked forward to this period; and in order to have the means of effecting a thorough change in his external appearance, and to be able to support himself after his return East, until he obtained some kind of employment, he had left nearly all his pay in the hands of the disbursing officer. It now amounted to nearly two hundred dollars.

It was in Santa Fe that Andrew obtained his discharge from the United States' service. This was soon after the conclusion of the peace with Mexico, and about the time when the first exciting news came of golden discoveries on the tributaries of the Sacramento.

On the day after Andrew received his discharge, and while making preparations for his journey eastward, a company, in which were several new recruits arrived from the Wachita. Among them he discovered a young man from P—, to whom he put the direct question.

"Do you know a Mr. Howland of your city?"

"Andrew Howland, the merchant?" inquired the young man, who was not over twenty-one years of age.

"Yes," returned Andrew, in a tone of affected indifference.

"His store is in the same block with my father's."

"Indeed! What is your father's name?"

The young man's eyes fell to the ground, and his face became overspread with crimson.

"Winters," he replied, at length recovering himself.

Andrew turned partly away to conceal the sudden emotion this intelligence had created. Mastering his feelings with a vigorous effort, he lifted his eyes to the countenance of the young man and at once recognized in him the brother of Emily. Restraining the eagerness he felt to press many questions, Andrew asked him about his journey from the last military post, and after getting a number of answers to which he scarcely listened, said—

"How long is it since you left P—?"

"About six months," replied young Winters.

"Do your friends know where you are?"

"No, indeed! Nor would I have them. So, please bear that in mind. I answered your question almost on the spur of the moment."

"Do you know anything about Mr. Howland or his family?" asked Andrew, without seeming to notice the young man's remark.

"Nothing very particular; only that the old gentleman failed in business about a year ago."

"Ah! How came that?"

"His son Edward broke him up."

"His son Edward?"

"Yes. The old man set him a going in business; but he soon run himself under, and his father into the bargain. He made a terrible bad failure of it."

"Who?"

"Edward Howland. He went off soon after, and they do say, carried his pockets full of money. And I imagine there is some truth in it. He wasn't exactly the clear grit. Some people called him a smooth-faced hypocrite, and I guess they were not very far wrong."

Andrew asked no more questions for some time, but sat, thoughtful, with his face so far turned away from the young man, that its expression could not be seen.

"Mrs. Howland is living, I presume?" said he, at length, in a tone as indifferent as he could assume; but which was, nevertheless, unsteady.

"Yes. She was living when I came away."

Andrew drew a quick breath, and then his laboring chest found relief in a long expiration.

"Poor old man! I'm sorry for him," came from his lips in a few moments afterwards. The tone was half indifferent, yet expressed some sympathy.

"Everybody seems sorry for him," said Winters. "It has broken him down very much. He looks ten years older."

"Is he entirely out of business?" asked Andrew.

"No; he is still going on; but he doesn't appear to do much. I think the family is poor. They've sold their handsome house, and are living in a much smaller one. I heard father say that Mr. Howland had received an extension from his creditors, but that he was too much crippled to be able to go through, and would, in the end, break down entirely."

There was another pause, and then Andrew changed the subject by asking the young man something about himself, and led on the conversation, from step to step, until he got him to mention the fact that he had a sister named Emily.

"Is she older than yourself?" inquired Andrew.

"Oh, yes. Some four years older," was replied.

"Married, of course," said Andrew.

The very effort he made to say this with seeming unconcern gave so unnatural an expression to his tone of voice, that young Winters looked at him with momentary surprise.

"No, she is not married," he answered.

"She's old enough," said Andrew, speaking now in a tone of more real indifference.

"Yes; but she'll probably die an old maid. She's had two or three good offers; but no one appears just to suit her fancy. Father was very angry about her rejecting a young man some two or three years ago, who afterwards disgraced himself, and broke the heart of a young creature who had been weak enough to marry him."

"Then I should say that your sister was a sensible girl," remarked Andrew, in a cheerful voice.

"Yes, she is a sensible girl; and, what is more, a good girl. Ah, me! I wish I were half as sensible and half as good."

With what a free motion did the heart of Andrew beat after receiving this intelligence!

"Is Mary Howland married?" he asked. He knew that she was, for he had seen the fact noticed in a newspaper.

"Yes; she married a Mr. Markland."

"Who is he?"

"I don't know much about, him. He's a teller in one of the banks."

"How did the family like her marriage?"

"Not at all. They don't visit."

"Indeed! Why?"

"Dear knows! Old Mr. Howland is a hard sort of a man when he takes up a prejudice against any one. He didn't like Markland, and said that Mary shouldn't marry him. She felt differently, and did marry him. The consequence was, that the old man said and did so much that was offensive, that he and Markland have had no intercourse since."

"Mary comes home, I suppose?"

"I rather think not. I believe that she and her father have not spoken in two years. At least, so I heard sister once say."

"That is bad! Poor man! He is unfortunate with his children."

Andrew, as he spoke, felt that he was unfortunate, and an emotion of pity stirred along the surface of his feelings.

"Indeed he is!" said Winters, who was disposed to be communicative. "But I presume it is a good deal his own fault. They say that his harsh treatment drove his oldest son from home."

"Ah?"

"Yes. He was a wild sort of a boy, and his father didn't show him any mercy. The consequence was, that instead of leading him into the right way, he drove him into the wrong way. He ran off from home a great while ago, and has never been heard from since. It is thought that he is dead. I once heard father say that, with all his faults, he was the best of the bunch."

Something interrupted the conversation of the two young men at this point, and they separated. A couple of hours afterward, as Andrew walked along one of the streets of Santa Fe, musing over the intelligence he had gleaned from young Winters, a fellow soldier, whose time of service had also just expired, met him, and said—

"You're not going back to the States, are you?"

"Such has been my intention," replied Andrew.

"I'm not going."

"I thought you were."

"I've altered my mind. A party sets off to-morrow for the gold regions of California, and I'm going with them."

"Indeed! That's a sudden change of resolution. But you don't believe all the stories you hear of this El Dorado?

"No, not all of them. But if even the half be true, there's a golden harvest to be reaped by all who put in the sickle."

"Yes, the half is encouraging enough," said Andrew, in a tone of abstraction. The fact is, since he had heard from home, his desire to return immediately was lessened. News of his father's altered circumstances had softened his feelings toward him very much, and created a strong desire to aid him in the extremity to which he had been reduced. But he had no ability to do this. All he possessed in the world was about two hundred dollars, and it would take at least half of this to pay his passage home. Already had his thoughts been reaching Westward, as the only point where, by any possibility, he could better his fortunes to an extent that would enable him to help his father. But there was so much of apparent romance in the stories that reached his ears, that he had many strong doubts as to even the main facts reported.

"You'd better join us," remarked the comrade.

"How many are going?" inquired Andrew.

"Seven. And we'd very much like to add you to the number."

"I'm really half-inclined to go with you," said Andrew, speaking with a good deal of animation in his voice.

"You'll never regret it," said the other. "Not only are the stories about an abundance of gold authentic, but I have good reasons for believing that the half has not been told. I talked with a man last night, who says that he knew of several instances where lumps of the precious metal, weighing several pounds, have been picked up. One man collected ten thousand dollars worth of lumps of pure gold in a week."

"That's a large story," replied Andrew, smiling.

"Perhaps so; but it is not all a fabrication. At any rate, I am off to this region, and my advice to you is, to join our little party."

"When do you start?

"To-morrow morning."

"I'll think about it," said Andrew Howland.

"You must think quickly," was answered. "There is no time to spare. It is but two hours to nightfall; and we are to be in the saddle by sunrise. So, if you conclude to join our party you have but small space left for preparation."

Andrew stood with his eyes upon the ground for nearly a minute; then looking up, he said, in a firm voice—

"I will go."

"And, my word for it, you'll never repent the decision. Gathering up lumps of gold by the peck is a quicker way to fortune than dragooning it at five dollars a month—ha?"

"My anticipations lie within a much narrower circle than yours," was quietly answered to this; "but one thing is certain, if gold is to be had in California for the mere digging, you may depend on Andrew Howland getting his share of the treasure."

"That's the spirit, my boy!" said the other, clapping him on the shoulder—"the very spirit of every member of our little party. And if we don't line our pockets with the precious stuff, it will be because none is to be found."

On the next morning, Andrew Howland started on his long and perilous journey for the region of gold, with a new impulse in his heart, and a hope in the future, such as, up to this time, he had never known. But it was not a mere selfish love of gold that was influencing him. He was acted on by a nobler feeling.

CHAPTER XII.

FROM the shock of his son's failure, Mr. Howland did not recover. In arranging with his own creditors, he had arranged to do too much, and consequently his reduced business went on under pressure of serious embarrassment. He had sold his house, and two other pieces of property, and was living at a very moderate expense; but all this did not avail, and he saw the steady approaches of total ruin.

One day, at a time when this conviction was pressing most heavily upon him, one of the creditors of Edward, who had lost a good deal by the young man, came into the store, and asked if he had heard lately from his son.

Mr. Howland replied he had not.

"He's in Mobile, I understand?" said the gentleman.

"I believe he is," returned Mr. Howland.

"A correspondent of mine writes that he is in business there, and seems to have plenty of money."

"It is only seeming, I presume," remarked Mr. Howland.

"He says that he has purchased a handsome piece of property there."

"It cannot be possible!" was ejaculated.

"I presume that my information is true. Now, my reason for communicating this fact to you is, that you may write to him, and demand, if he have money to invest, that he refund to you a portion of what you have paid for him, and thus save you from the greater difficulties that I too plainly see gathering around you, and out of which I do not think it is possible for you to come unaided."

"No, sir," was the reply of Mr. Howland, as he slowly shook his head. "If he have money, it is ill-gotten, and I cannot share it. He owes you, write to him, and demand a payment of the debt."

"I am willing to yield my right in your favor, Mr. Howland. In your present extremity, you can make an appeal that it will be impossible for him to withstand. He may not dream of the position in which you are placed; and it is due to him that you inform him thereof. It will give him an opportunity to act above an evil and selfish spirit, and this action may be in him the beginning of a better state."

But the father shook his head again.

"Mr. Howland," said the other "you owe it to your son to put it in his power to act from a better principle than the one that now appears to govern him. Let him know of your great extremity, and he may compel himself to act against the selfish cupidities by which he is too plainly governed. Such action, done in violence of evil affections, may be to him the beginning of a better life. All things originate in small beginnings. There must first be a point of influx for good, as well as for bad principles. Sow this seed in your son's mind, and it may germinate, and grow into a plant of honesty."

Mr. Howland heaved a deep sigh, as he answered—

"This is presenting the subject in a new light; I will think about it."

"May you think about it to good purpose," replied the friend, earnestly.

This communication disturbed Mr. Howland greatly. He had too many good reasons for doubting his son's integrity of character; but he was not prepared to hear of such deliberate and cruel dishonesty as this. It was but another name for robbery—a robbery, even to the ruin of his own father.

"I will demand restitution!" said the old man, impatiently, as his mind dwelt longer and longer on the subject, and his feelings grew more and more indignant. From the thought of any appeal on the ground of humanity, he revolted. It was something entirely out of keeping with his peculiar character. He could not bend to this.

So Mr. Howland wrote a pretty strong letter to his son, in which he set forth in terse language the facts he had heard, and demanded as a right, that restitution be at once made.

Weeks passed and no answer to this demand was received. In the meantime, another crisis in the affairs of Mr. Howland was rapidly approaching. Unless aid were received from some quarter, he must sink utterly prostrate under the pressure that was upon him, and again fail to meet the honorable engagements that he had made. When that crisis came, he would fall to rise no more.

Ten days only remained, and then there would come a succession of payments, amounting in all to over five thousand dollars. To meet these payments unaided, would be impossible; and there was no one now to aid the reduced and sinking merchant. There was not a friend to whom he could go for aid so substantial as was now required, for most of his business friends had already suffered to some extent by his failure, and were not in the least inclined to risk anything farther on one whose position was known to be extremely doubtful.

The nearer this second crisis came, and the more distinctly Mr. Howland was able to see its painful features, the more did his heart shrink from encountering a disaster that would involve all his worldly affairs in hopeless ruin.

In this strait, the mind of Mr. Howland kept turning, involuntarily, toward his son Edward, as toward the only resource left him on the earth; but ever as it turned thus, something in him revolted at the idea, and he strove to push it from his thoughts. He could not do this, however, for it was the straw on the surface of the waters in which he felt himself sinking.

Painfully, and with a sense of deep humiliation, did Mr. Howland at length bring himself up to the point of writing again to his son. As everything depended on the effect of this second letter, he went down into a still lower deep of humiliation, and after representing in the most vivid colors the extremity to which he was reduced, begged him, if a spark of humanity remained in his bosom, to send him the aid he needed.

With a trembling hope did the father wait, day after day, for an answer to this letter. Time passed on, and the ninth day since its transmission came and yet there was no reply.

Nervously anxious was Mr. Howland on the morning of the tenth day, for if no help came then, it was all over with him. His note for fifteen hundred dollars fell due, and must be lifted ere the stroke of three, or the end with him had come.

A few mouthfuls of food were taken at breakfast, and then Mr. Howland hurried away to the Post Office, his heart fluttering with fear and expectation. A few moments, and he would know his fate. As he came in sight of the long row of boxes, his eyes glanced eagerly toward the one in which his letters were filed up. There was something in it. In a tone of forced composure, he called out the number of his box, and received from the clerk two letters. He glanced at the post-mark of one, and read—"New York," and at the other, and saw—"Boston." For a moment or two his breath was suspended, and his knees smote together. Then he moved away, slowly, with such a pressure on his feelings that the weight was reproduced on his physical system, and he walked with difficulty.

The letters were from business correspondents, and in no way affected the position of extremity he occupied. For a greater part of the morning Mr. Howland sat musing at his desk, in a kind of dreamy abstraction. All effort was felt to be useless, and he made none. At dinner time he went home, and sat at the table, silent and gloomy; but he scarcely tasted food. After the meal, he returned to his store—a faint hope springing up in his mind that Edward might have submitted the aid he had asked for so humbly by private hand, or through some broker in the city, and that it would yet arrive in time to save him. Alas! this proved a vain hope. Three o'clock came, and the unredeemed note still lay in bank.

"It is all over!" murmured the unhappy man, as like the strokes of a hammer upon his heart fell the three distinct chimes that rung the knell of his business life.

Taking up a newspaper, and affecting to read, Mr. Howland sat for nearly an hour awaiting the notorial visit, which seemed long delayed. At last he saw a man enter and come walking back toward the desk at which he sat. Not doubting but that it was the Notary, he was preparing to answer—"I can't take it, up," when a well-dressed stranger, with a dark, sun-burnt, countenance that had in it many familiar lines, passed before him, and fixed his eyes with an earnest look upon his face. For a few moments the two men regarded each other in silence, and then the stranger reached out his hand and uttered the single word—

"Father!"

"Andrew!" responded Mr. Howland, catching eagerly hold of the offered hand; "Andrew! my son! my son! are you yet alive?"

The great deep of the old man's heart was suddenly broken up, and he was overwhelmed by the rising floods of emotion. His lips quivered; there was a convulsive play of all the muscles of his face; and then large tears came slowly over his cheeks. The man of iron will was melted down; he wept like a child, and his son wept with him.

Scarcely had the first strong emotions created by this meeting exhausted themselves, when another person entered the store, and advanced to where the father and son were standing. He held a small slip of paper in his hand, and as he came up to Mr. Howland, he said, holding up the piece of paper—

"Your note for fifteen hundred dollars remains unpaid."

"I'm sorry, but I can't lift it," replied Mr. Howland, in a low voice that he wished not to reach the ear of his son; but Andrew heard the answer distinctly, and instantly drawing a large pocket book from his pocket, took out a roll of bank bills which he reached to his father, saying, as he did so—

"Take what you want. How timely has been my arrival!"

"My heart blesses you, my son, for this generous tender of aid in a great extremity," said Mr. Howland in a trembling voice, as he pushed back the roll of money. "But a crisis in my affairs has just arrived, and the lifting of this note will not save me."

"How much will save you?" asked Andrew.

"I must have five or six thousand dollars in as many days," replied Mr. Howland.

"This package of money will serve you then, for it contains ten thousand dollars," said Andrew. "Take it."

"I cannot rob you thus," returned Mr. Howland, in a broken voice, as he still drew back.

"Let me have that note, my friend." Andrew now turned to the Notary, who did not hesitate to exchange the merchant's promise to pay, for three five hundred dollar bills of a solvent bank.

A brief but earnest and affectionate interview then took place between Andrew and his father, which closed with a request from the former that he might be permitted to see his mother alone, and spend with her the few hours that remained until evening, before the latter joined them.

CHAPTER XIII.

IT is nine years since Mrs. Howland looked her last look on her wayward, wandering boy, and eight years since any tidings came from him to bless her yearning heart. She appears older by almost twenty years, and moves about with a quiet drooping air, as if her heart were releasing itself from its hold on earthly objects, and reaching out its tendrils for a higher and surer support. With the exception of Martha, the youngest, all her children have given her trouble. Scarcely one of the sweet hopes cherished by her heart, when they first lay in helpless innocence upon her bosom, have been realized. Disappointment—disappointment—has come at almost every step of her married life. The iron hand of her husband has crushed almost every thing. Ah! how often and often, as she breathed the chilling air of her own household, where all was constrained propriety, would her heart go back to the sunny home in which were passed the happy days of girlhood, and wish that something of the wisdom and gentleness that marked her father's intercourse with his children could be transferred to her uncompromising husband. But that was a vain wish. The two men had been cast in far different moulds.

Martha, now in her eighteenth year, was more like her mother than any of the children, and but for the light of her presence Mrs. Howland could hardly have kept her head above the waters that were rushing around her. Toward Martha the conduct of her father had, from the first, been of a mild character compared with his action toward the other children; and this received a still farther modification, when it become apparent even to himself, that by his hardness he had estranged the affections of his elder children, and driven them away. Gentle and loving in all her actions, she gradually won her way more and more deeply into the heart of her father, until she acquired a great influence over him. This influence she had tried to make effectual in bringing about a reconciliation between him and her sister's husband; but, up to this time, her good offices were not successful. The old man's prejudices remained strong—he was not prepared to yield; and Markland's self-love having been deeply wounded by Mr. Howland, he was not disposed to make any advances toward healing the breach that existed. As for Mary, she cherished too deeply the remembrance of her father's unbending severity toward his children—in fact his iron hand had well nigh crushed affection out of her heart—to feel much inclined to use any influence with her husband. And so the separation, unpleasant and often painful to both parties, continued. To Mrs. Howland it was a source of constant affliction. Much had she done toward affecting a reconciliation; but the materials upon which she tried to impress something of her own gentle and forgiving spirit were of too hard a nature.

On the afternoon of the day on which Andrew returned so unexpectedly, almost like one rising from the dead, Mrs. Howland was alone, Martha having gone out to visit a friend. She was sitting in her chamber thinking of the long absent one—she had thought of him a great deal of late—when she heard the street door open and shut, and then there came the sound of a man's feet along the passage. She bent her head and listened. It was not the sound of her husband's feet—she knew his tread too well. Soon the man, whoever he was, commenced ascending the stairs; then he came toward her door, and then there was a gentle tap. The heart of Mrs. Howland was, by this time, beating violently. A moment or two passed before she had presence of mind sufficient to go to the door and open it.

"Andrew! Andrew! Oh, Andrew, my son!" she cried, in a glad, eager voice, the instant her eyes rested on the fine figure of a tall, sun-burnt man, and as she spoke, she flung her arms around his neck, and kissed him with all the fondness of a mother caressing her babe.

"Mother! dear, dear mother!" came sobbing from the lips of Andrew, as he returned her embrace fervently.

"Am I dreaming? or, is this all really so?" murmured the happy mother, pushing her son from her, yet clinging to him with an earnest grasp, and gazing fondly upon his face.

"It is no dream, mother," returned Andrew, "but a glad reality. After a long, long absence I have come back."

"Long—long! Oh, it has been an age, my son! How could you? But hush, my chiding heart! My wandering one has returned, and I will ask no questions as to his absence. Enough that I look upon his face again."

Andrew now led his mother to a seat, and taking one beside her, while he still held her hand tightly, and gazed with a look of tenderness into her face, said—

"You have grown old in nine years, mother; older than I had thought."

"Do you wonder at it, my son?" significantly inquired Mrs. Howland.

"I ought not to wonder, perhaps," replied Andrew, a touch of sadness in his voice. "There is such a thing as living too fast for time."

"You may well say that," answered Mrs. Howland, with visible emotion, "Years are sometimes crowded into as many days. This has been my own experience."

Both were now silent for a little while.

"And how are all the rest, mother?" asked Andrew, in a more animated voice.

"Your father has failed a good deal of late," replied Mrs. Howland, as she partly averted her eyes, doubtful as to the effect such reference might have.

"He has failed almost as much as you have, mother," was the unexpected reply. "I saw him a little while ago."

"Did you!" ejaculated Mrs. Howland, a light of pleasure and surprise breaking over her face.

"Yes; I called first at his store."

"I'm glad you did. Poor man! He has had his own troubles, and, I'm afraid, is falling into difficulties again. He has looked very unhappy for a week or two. Last night I hardly think he slept an hour at a time, and to-day he scarcely tasted food."

"I found him in trouble," said Andrew, "and fortunately was able to give him the relief he needed."

Mrs. Howland looked wonderingly into her son's face.

"I have not come back empty-handed, mother," said Andrew. "A year ago, when thousands of miles from home, I heard of father's troubles. I was about returning to see you all again, and to make P—my future abiding place, if I could find any honest employment; but this intelligence caused me to change my mind. News had just been received of the wonderful discoveries of gold in California, and I said to myself, 'If there is gold to be had there, I will find it.' I was not thinking of myself when I made this resolution, but of you and father. In this spirit I made the long and wearisome overland journey, and for more than eight, months worked amid the golden sands of that far off region. And my labor was not in vain. I accumulated a large amount of grains and lumps of the precious metal, and then hurried homeward to lay the treasures at your feet. Happily, I arrived at the most fitting time."

Mrs. Howland was deeply affected by this relation, so strange and so unlooked for in every particular.

"And now, mother, what of Mary?" said Andrew, before time was given for any remark upon this brief narrative. "Has she and her husband yet been reconciled to father?"

"No; and my heart has grown faint with hope deferred in relation to this matter. I think Mary's husband is too unyielding. Your father, I know, regrets the unkind opposition he made to their marriage; and has seen many good reasons for changing his opinion of Mr. Markland's character. But you know his unbending disposition. If they would yield a little—if they would only make the first step toward a reconciliation, he would be softened in a moment. And then, oh, how much happier would all be!"

"They must yield; they must take the first step," said Andrew, rising from his chair.

"That reconciliation would be the top sheaf of my happiness, today," replied Mrs. Howland.

"It shall crown your rejoicing," said Andrew, in a positive tone. "Where do they live?"

Mrs. Howland gave the direction asked by her son, who departed immediately on his errand of good will.

For a time after Andrew left the store of his father, Mr. Howland sat half bewildered by the strange occurrence that had just taken place, while his heart felt emotions of tenderness going deeper and deeper toward its centre. Though confessed to no one, he had felt greatly troubled in regard to the iron discipline to which he had subjected his wayward boy, and had tried for years, but in vain, to force from his mind the conviction that upon his own head rested the sin of his ruin. Long since had he given him up as lost to this world, and, he sadly feared, lost in the next. To have him return, as he did, without even a foreshadowing sign of his coming, was an event that completely broke down his feelings. Moreover, he was touched by the spirit in which his son came back; a spirit of practical forgiveness; the first act flowing from which was the conference of a great benefit.

"There was good in the boy," sighed the old man, as he mused on what had just occurred. "Alas! that it should have been so long overshadowed. A milder course might have done better. Ah, me! we are weak and shortsighted mortals."

Mr. Howland remained in his store until the late mails were distributed at the post-office, when, unexpectedly, a letter came from Edward. It contained a draft for a thousand dollars, and was in these words—

"DEAR FATHER—I received your two letters. To the first returned no answer; I need hardly give you the reason. It was a hard, harsh, insulting letter, charging me with extensive frauds on you and others, assuming that I was in possession of large sums of money thus obtained, and imperiously demanding restitution. As to your sources of information, I know nothing; but I trust, that before you take such stories for granted, you will, at least, look well to their authenticity. Your second letter was in a different tone, and awoke in me a far different spirit from that awakened by the one first received. I am pained to hear of your great embarrassment, which I did not anticipate. I thought that the extension of time you received, would enable you to meet all demands, and deeply regret that such has not proved to be the case. Enclosed, I send you a draft for one thousand dollars, which I have raised with great difficulty; I wish, for your sake, that it were ten times the amount. But it is the best I can do. When I came here I had about fifteen hundred dollars in money; upon this I commenced business, and have done tolerably well, but I am still on the steep up-hill side, and it is far from certain whether I will go up or down from the point I now occupy. Give my love to mother and Martha,

Affectionately yours,
EDWARD."

Mr. Howland mused for some time after receiving the letter; then he turned to his desk, and wrote briefly, as follows—

"MY DEAR SON—I have your letter enclosing a draft for one thousand dollars. I thank you for the remittance, but, happily, have received aid from an unexpected quarter, and do not now need the money. With this I return the draft you sent. I regret any injustice I may have done you in a former letter, and hope you will forgive a too warm expression of my feelings.

Yours, &c.,
ANDREW HOWLAND."

This letter was dispatched by the Southern mail, and then Mr. Howland turned his steps homeward. He felt strangely. There was a pressure on his bosom; but it was not the pressure of trouble that had rested upon it so long, but a pressure of conflicting emotions, all tending to soften and subdue his feelings, to bend the iron man, and to mould his spirit into a new and better form. With a lively pleasure was he looking forward to the second meeting with Andrew in the presence of his mother, but he did not know how great a pleasure, beyond his anticipations, was in store for him.

On arriving at his house, Mr. Howland opened the door and went in. He had passed along the entry but a few paces, when some one stepped from the parlor. He paused, and looked up. It was his daughter Mary who stood before him. In her arms was a sweet little girl, and on her face was a smile, the warmth and light of which were on his heart in an instant.

"Father!"

It was the only word she uttered. The tone of her voice, and the expression of her face told all he wished to know.

"My dear child!" fell warmly from the lips of Mr. Howland, as he grasped his daughter's hand, and then kissed tenderly both her own lips and those of her babe.

"Dear father!" murmured Mary, as she leaned her head, in tears, upon his breast.

At this moment there was a movement of feet in the parlor, and the husband of Mary presented himself. An open, frank, forgiving expression was on his face, as he came forward and offered his hand, which was instantly seized by Mr. Howland, in a hearty pressure. Andrew and his mother joined the group, and, with smiles and pleasant words, made perfect the sphere of happiness.

"My children," said Mr. Howland, at length, speaking in a trembling voice, "my cup is full to-night. I must leave you a little while, or it will run over."

And saying this, he gently disengaged himself, and passed up to his chamber, where he remained alone for over half an hour. When he joined the family, his manner was greatly subdued, and in his speech there was a softness which none had known before.

In the glad reunion of that evening, how many heart-wounds were healed, how many old scars covered over and hidden!

CHAPTER XIV.

SHOCKED as was Emily Winters at the sight of Andrew, bleeding in the hands of the watchman, and by the subsequent newspaper report of his bad conduct; and estranged from her early regard for him, as she had been, by these and other things that she had heard, the young girl could not entirely banish from her mind the image of the boy who had been to her so gentle and affectionate since the early and innocent days of childhood. In spite of all her efforts to turn her thoughts away from him, they were ever turning toward him; and, as time passed on, and his long absence left all in doubt concerning his fate, his memory became to her something like a hallowed thing.

In passing on to the estate of womanhood, Emily, who possessed more than common beauty, attracted admirers, and from two or three of these she received offers of marriage. But in each case the suitor had failed to win her heart, and she was too true a woman to give her hand to any one unless her heart could go also.

In at least one case her father took sides with the lover, and urged his suit with a degree of feeling that resulted in a partial estrangement of affection. But he afterward had cause to be well satisfied with Emily's decision in the case.

On the morning that had succeeded the day of Andrew Howland's return to P—, Emily Winters, who had long since ceased to think of the young man as alive, was informed that a gentleman had called, and wished to see her.

"Who is he?" was the natural inquiry.

"I don't know," replied the servant.

"You should have asked his name."

"I did so, but he said that it was no matter."

After making some slight change in her dress, Emily went down to the parlor. As she entered, a gentleman arose and advanced a few steps toward her.

"Miss Winters!" said he, while he fixed his eyes intently on her face.

The young lady bowed slightly in return, while she looked at him inquiringly.

"You don't know me?" said the stranger, with perceptible disappointment in his voice.

Emily dropped her eyes for a moment to the floor, and then lifted them again to his countenance. There was a gentle suffusion on her face, as she slowly shook her head.

"I have seen you before," she remarked, "but I cannot, at this moment, tell where."

"Years have passed since we met," replied the stranger, with something of sadness in his voice; "but I had hoped you would not forget me."

As he spoke, he came nearer, and held out his hand, which Emily did not hesitate to take.

At the moment of this contact, a light flashed on the maiden's face, and she exclaimed, with sudden emotion—

"Andrew Howland! Can it be?"

And she stepped back a pace or two, and sunk upon a chair. Andrew did not relinquish her hand, but sat down by her side, replying, as he did so—

"Yes, Emily, it is even so. After a long, long absence, I have come back to my old home, wiser and better, I trust, than when I went away."

It was some time before Emily looked up or replied; but she did not make a motion to withdraw the hand which Andrew held with no slight pressure.

"How often, Emily," continued Andrew, seeing that she remained silent, "have I thought of the sweet hours we spent together as children—hours, too often, of stolen delight. Their remembrance has, many a time, saved me from evil when strongly tempted. But for that, and the memory of my mother, I should long since have become a castaway on the ocean of life."

The voice of Andrew became tremulous as he uttered the last sentence. It was then that Emily raised her eyes from the floor, gently withdrawing her hand at the same time, and fixed them upon his face. His words had sent her thoughts back to the old time when they were children together, and when, to be within him, was one of her highest pleasures; and, not only that, his words and tones had reached her heart, and awakened therein an echo.

"It is a long time since you went away," said Emily. "A very long time."

"Yes; it is a long time. But, the weary slow-passing years are ended, and I am back again among early scenes and old friends, and back, I trust, to remain."

"How is your mother?" inquired Emily, after a slight pause.

"I found her much changed—older by twice the number of years that have elapsed since I went away."

But all that passed between Andrew Howland and Emily Winters in the hour they spent together at this first meeting, after so long an absence, we cannot write. For a time, their intercourse was marked by a reserve and embarrassment on the part of Emily; but this insensibly wore off, and, ere the young man went away, their hearts, if not their lips, had spoken to each other almost as freely as in the days of childhood.

Not many months elapsed ere the tender regard that was spontaneously awakened in their bosoms when children, and which had never ceased to exist, led them into a true marriage union, to which no one raised even a whisper of opposition. Almost at the very time that Andrew was holding his first interview with Emily, Mr. Winters was listening to a brief account of his return, with some of the pleasing incidents immediately attendant thereon. In a meeting with the young man shortly afterward, he was prepossessed in his favor, and when he saw that he was disposed to renew the old intimate relations with Emily, he did not in the least object.

Thus, after a lapse of over twenty-five years, two families, each possessed of substantial virtues, and with social qualities forming a plane for reciprocal good feeling, but which had been forced apart by the narrow prejudice and iron will of Mr. Howland, came together in a marriage of two of its members. Alas! how much of wrong and suffering appertained to that long period during which they were thus held apart! How many scars from heart-wounds were left; and these not always painless!

Can any summing up of the causes and consequences set forth in our story give force to the lessons it teaches? We think not; and therefore leave it with the reader to do its own work.